More Critical Praise for *The Perfume Burned His Eyes*

"Imperioli's book follows a Queens teen named Matthew as his shattered family moves from Jackson Heights to Manhattan, where he finds an unlikely mentor in a drug-addled Lou Reed."
—*New York Post*

"Compelling . . . Lou Reed appears as a major character; he's an unlikely father figure to the teenage protagonist, Matthew, who's trying to find himself in 1976 Manhattan. The iconoclastic—and at the time, troubled—rocker inspires Matthew artistically, even as he coaxes him to walk on the wild side." —*Maclean's*

"Vividly imagined, compelling, and sympathetic, *The Perfume Burned His Eyes* convinces with the force of its emotional intensity."
—Joyce Carol Oates

"This coming-of-age narrative is a fearless, towering inferno burning with raw truthfulness, stunning surprises, thrills, poetic writing, and an odyssey not just to be read, but reckoned with."
—Richard Lewis, comedian, author of *The Other Great Depression*

"Michael Imperioli discovers a whole new demimonde in his journey from Queens to the hideaways and hell-a-ways of Manhattan. It's streetwise romp through an underworld of bizarre characters desperate to find their own transcendence, written with affection, wit, and telepathic understanding."

nny Kaye, musician and author

T0026536

"Even though Reed looms large throughout—the novel even takes its title from Reed's 'Romeo Had Juliette,' from his 1989 solo album *New York*—the book is much less about him and more about Matthew's own journey through adolescence in the seedier corners of 1970s New York." —*Stereogum*

"An edgy coming-of-age romp set in New York City prominently featuring the 'character' of rocker Lou Reed." —*Parade*

"[Imperioli's] debut novel, *The Perfume Burned His Eyes*, not only deserves an award for best title, but has garnered praise from Joyce Carol Oates . . . This should come as no surprise . . . Bravo!"
—*Santa Barbara Magazine*

"It has been a long time since I have regarded the prospect of taking up a new first novel other than with dull dread and a sardonic snort of rightfully prejudicial dismissal. Then I happened on this one: the kind of bird you don't see anymore in the kind of sky you don't see anymore. Mr. Imperioli can write, and he has given us a book—that most outmoded of handheld devices, devoid of all apps—that brings a rare and welcome breeze of imagination and wit." —Nick Tosches, author of *Under Tiberius*

"Touching, hilarious, heartfelt, and poetic, with an ending that is crushing, bruising, beautiful . . . Unpredictable and sweet as well, this is a unique accomplishment."
—Lydia Lunch, author of *Will Work for Drugs*

"[Imperioli] captured the setting, the times, and the coming of age beautifully. It was a compelling read." —*Cyberlibrarian*

"Imperioli's lived-in details about the city help make the world feel realistic . . . [The novel] is an immersive trip into its narrator's memories of a turbulent time. Some fictional trips into 1970s New York abound with nostalgia; this novel memorably opts for grit and heartbreak."   —*Kirkus Reviews*

"Imperioli delivers a spot-on coming-of-age novel . . . A winner."
                                                    —*Library Journal*

"Imperioli makes his literary debut with *The Perfume Burned His Eyes*, a novel in which sixteen-year-old narrator Matthew becomes enmeshed with the late rock legend Lou Reed and his trans muse Rachel."   —*Bay Area Reporter*

"Imperioli does a masterful job with this work, and with his influences from the acting world, it reads vividly, like a movie."
                                                    —*Brooklyn Digest*

"*The Perfume Burned His Eyes* shook me up in a way a book hasn't since my twenties. I found myself questioning the narrative I have built for myself in order to survive as an artist and a parent. It threw me back to being an awkward teenager in love, and destroyed some of the scaffolding of false memories I had built . . . Imperioli's book is gentle, pure, perverse, and devastating. It delves intimately into the psyche of what all great artists are made of."

        —Nick Sandow, actor (*Orange Is the New Black*), filmmaker

David Imperioli

Michael Imperioli is best known for his starring role as Christopher Moltisanti in the acclaimed TV series *The Sopranos*—which earned him a Best Supporting Actor Emmy Award—and currently plays a lead role on season two of HBO's *The White Lotus*. He wrote five episodes of *The Sopranos*; was coscreenwriter of the film *Summer of Sam*, directed by Spike Lee; and was anthologized in *The Nicotine Chronicles*, edited by Lee Child. Imperioli has appeared in six of Spike Lee's films and has also acted in films by Martin Scorsese, Abel Ferrara, Walter Hill, Peter Jackson, and the Hughes Brothers. He cohosted the rewatch podcast *Talking Sopranos* with his *Sopranos* costar Steve Schirripa, with whom he also penned the best-selling book *Woke Up This Morning: The Definitive Oral History of The Sopranos*. Additionally, Imperioli is a singer and guitarist in the band ZOPA. Follow him on Instagram: @realmichaelimperioli.

THE PERFUME BURNED HIS EYES

THE PERFUME BURNED HIS EYES

A NOVEL BY
MICHAEL IMPERIOLI

BROOKLYN, NEW YORK

This is a work of fiction. While some characters portrayed here have counterparts among real individuals, living or dead, all of the names, characters, places, and incidents are either the product of the author's imagination or are used fictitiously.

Cover photo: Joseph Sterling, *The Age of Adolescence*, 1959–64, copyright Deborah Sterling, courtesy of the Stephen Daiter Gallery.

Published by Akashic Books
©2018, 2022 Michael Imperioli

Paperback ISBN: 978-1-63614-069-8
Hardcover ISBN: 978-1-61775-620-7
Library of Congress Control Number: 2017956424

All rights reserved
First paperback printing

Akashic Books
Brooklyn, New York
Instagram, Twitter, Facebook: AkashicBooks
E-mail: info@akashicbooks.com
Website: www.akashicbooks.com

to Victoria, for a love inconceivable

to my children, for being my greatest teachers

I've known you for years. Everyone says you were beautiful when you were young, but I want to tell you I think you're more beautiful now than then. Rather than your face as a young woman, I prefer your face as it is now. Ravaged.
—from Marguerite Duras, *The Lover*

one

On this, the 24th of July in the year 1977, in the Borough of Manhattan of the State of New York, being of sound mind and body, I . . .

This was originally meant to be a last will and testament type of thing, maybe it still will be at some point. I don't know. Right now I just want to get as much as I can down on paper. I have been praised for this effort and told that it may bring me some clarity. I was not aware I lacked clarity or that the events described here were unclear, but that is what I have been told by people who are supposed to know about such things.

I have also been informed that this is a very difficult time in one's life and it's not uncommon for folks my age to find themselves in similar situations. This brings me no comfort, and I feel it is important for me to state that for the record. Even if the record is a shitty little ninety-nine-cent notebook.

With this in mind, I would like to start at the most logical beginning. Although to be technical, dear sirs or madams, my birth would be the most formal or official beginning, and even further we could trace things back to my parents—how they met, their courtship and marriage, my conception . . . But I will spare you all those gory details and jump to the year when shit started to happen and people died and life as I knew it altered itself beyond recognition.

My parents split up a few days after the new year began so my dad hit the road in his shit-brown '72 Chrysler Newport. He had three garbage bags of clothes in the trunk and not much else.

I would never see him again.

In June, the day after I finished my sophomore year of high school, we found out he was dead. Legend has it that he checked out in an LA freeway pile-up that may or may not have been his fault. The facts of the terrible accident were never completely explained to me but in my gut I know it was him.

He was a reckless man who always let his emotions get the best of him and denied himself nothing. Driving at speeds over 110 miles an hour chasing down someone who dared to cut him off. Fucking half the women in Jackson Heights. Blowing eight thousand dollars of the family fortune on a lock at Belmont. I vowed I would never be an unfaithful husband, infidelity being something that I find unforgivable and repulsive. I also swore that when I eventually drove a car I would be patient and calm behind the wheel. I have yet to learn to drive nor have I ever placed a bet.

There was no funeral but my mother insisted I go to church with her one Friday to say a prayer in his honor. I went with her but I refused to say the prayer. Not after all the shit he put my mother through. Not after the disgrace and indignity she suffered on his watch. She deserved much better.

From what I could gather through eavesdropping, my mother would not accept possession of his ashes, despite her still being his legal wife. My dad had cut off all ties with his sister years ago, and she was his only living immediate family besides me and Mom. But Aunt Yol, short for Yolanda, was a fall-down drunk and a professional whore who lived out of a car in Seattle or Portland or some Pacific Northwest territory and nobody was able to track her down.

I have no idea where his remains wound up nor do I care in the least.

two

I spent the first few weeks of that summer in my friend Willie's attic watching him smoke pot while listening to Pink Floyd's *Wish You Were Here*. Please do not read anything into that title; it was my album but I assure you I did not wish my dad was here or anywhere. I was fine with wherever he was.

Willie was my best friend at the time. He was also a big fat fuck. Like really very fat. Slob fat.

To maintain his level of obesity, every night around nine or nine thirty we'd walk over to Christy's on Northern Boulevard and eat cheeseburgers. Willie would sometimes eat two, but usually he would eat three. With double cheese, bacon, and fries. And one or two vanilla milkshakes. His record was four burgers, four orders of fries, and four milkshakes. This triumphant milestone of human achievement was reached on the *fourth* of July that same summer. Willie considered it an act of high patriotism.

Each time we went to Christy's, I would hope that we would luck into the-waitress-with-the-long-red-hair's station. I had a huge crush on her. One night, after we ordered our food I tried to strike up a conversation with her. I asked if she was just beginning her shift or if she was finishing up for the night. She didn't really answer me, she just smiled and said, "Cute," kind of under her breath.

I got hot and my face must have flushed red. I had given myself away; cards on the table. She knew how I felt now and I was glad.

This was a much bigger moment than it seems because it was so out of character for me. I was very, very shy around girls my age and downright petrified of older girls, even if they were only juniors or seniors at school. This was a whole other league: the-waitress-with-the-long-red-hair was in her mid-to-late twenties. She was a *woman*.

I don't know where the courage came from. Maybe all the stuff with my dad had given birth to a *fuck it* kind of attitude in me. I'm not really sure.

When she walked away from the table Willie was staring at me with his fat mouth big and dumb and open. It looked like a baby's mouth that had grown to premature adulthood through some sick, unholy scientific experiment. His tongue was wet and swollen. I assumed he was hungry and wondered if that's how his tongue always looked on an empty stomach.

I had never told Willie that I liked her or thought she was hot. She had never come up in conversation and the times she waited on us in the past I stayed cool and composed. Willie stared at me and I noticed that even his eyelids were fat. He looked at me, gargantuan mouth all slack, then craned his neck to look at her. She was behind the counter calling out our order to the little cook with the big mustache. Willie turned the column of flesh beneath his head back at me.

A high-pitched "Ha" came out of his hippo mouth, only it wasn't really a "Ha," it was more like an "Ah." Whatever it was, it was a laugh, specifically the kind of laugh you make when you want somebody to feel like an idiot.

"Don't tell me you like her."

I didn't say anything in return.

"She's hideous." This from an acne-picking sixteen-year-old, wide as he was tall. He looked at her again, then at me, and repeated: "She's hideous."

It was those two words that made me hate Willie forever. It was also those same two words that made me realize what a moron I had been hanging out with and that I owed it to myself to seek out some friends who had a brain that at the very least functioned with a standard level of human intelligence.

The-waitress-with-the-long-red-hair was beautiful. There's no doubt in my mind that she could have been in magazines or on television instead of filling the troughs of adolescent swine like Willie. She was a knockout; her appearance unique and unconventional. Tall with bold features, like the Greeks and Romans. A classical beauty. Special.

"Look at her eyes . . . she's fucking bug-eyed. I think it's a birth defect. Maybe even a thalidomide case . . . I'd check her for flippers."

He finally closed his mouth. He looked like a cheap comedian waiting for the audience to laugh. I wanted to punch the shit-eating smile right off his face. Willie was so fucking stupid. She had incredible eyes. They were big and blue and round. And when she looked at you they grabbed you and held you and said so much. Even if it was just for a second.

I was quiet for a long time. I just sat there poking the ice in my Coke.

"She's also like forty years old, Matt. She can change your diapers." He shook his head and let out another high pitched "Ha" or "Ah" or whatever the fuck it was.

My ears felt very warm. They must have been bright red. I just kept peering down at my Coke, playing with the straw, pushing the ice around my glass.

"To be honest, she's quite mannish. I wouldn't be surprised if she's got a cock and balls."

I never wanted to see Willie again. I wanted to

grab the chicken drumsticks from the table of the next booth and shove them down Willie's throat. I'd hold them in place till he turned blue then force him to apologize to the-waitress-with-the-long-red-hair. But I just sat there and chewed on some ice.

She brought us our dinner. It was a three-burger night for Willie. I couldn't look at her and I sure as fuck couldn't look at Willie. He had this smug smirk across his face. He could barely contain himself. After she put our food on the table she paused for a second—I think she was waiting for me to look at her. I'm sure Willie was waiting for me to look at her too.

"Do you boys have everything you need?"

Willie snorted through his nose and coughed up some milkshake. Then he looked up at her. "I'm fine but my friend here may need something. Do you need anything, Matthew?"

He never called me Matthew. My head and neck were on fire and my legs were shaking. I shook my head; no, I didn't need anything except to smash this whole plate over my best friend's head and watch him bleed to death, buried in cheeseburgers, ketchup, and french fries.

"Okay then, enjoy your burgers."

She walked away and Willie burst into laughter. His head was bobbing up and down like the blow-up

Bozo punching bag I had when I was little. You'd punch him as hard as you could and he'd hit the floor and come back up only to get punched hard again. If only . . .

I was hoping his bobbing head would land his face right into his food and that it would be scalding hot and cook the flesh right off, leaving it sitting on his dish like bacon; but no such luck. His laughter subsided and he started doing what he did best: stuffing his mouth with cheeseburger.

It was always unpleasant to watch him eat but that night it was unbearable. He always chewed with his mouth open and made these disgusting smacking sounds as his tongue sucked the food off the roof of his mouth. I was sure I was going to puke any second.

"You eat like a cow."

I couldn't believe the words came out of my mouth. I am not a very confrontational person. I usually let things go, but something had happened to me. The *fuck it* thing had definitely begun to take over.

"And you know less about women than I do, and I admit I know hardly anything. She's a beautiful woman but you're just too stupid to see that."

Willie stopped chewing. He closed his mouth.

I was on a roll and kept going: "You have shitty taste in music . . . and you laugh like a little girl."

He looked at me with surprise, as if he wasn't sure if I was joking or not. I saw a little fear cross his eyes. Then he took a huge bite of cheeseburger and started chewing with his mouth wide open. Smacking the food between his palate and tongue in a loud, exaggerated way and staring right at me. Food flew from his mouth onto my plate.

And then I did it. I reached across the booth, grabbed the back of his head, and slammed his face into his plateful of food. He let out a muffled shriek, a very feminine-sounding cry. I didn't let him pull his head back up for a few seconds. When he finally surfaced his face was smeared with grease, cheese, and ketchup, and there were fries stuck to his nose.

It was beautiful. A work of art worthy of Pollock or Picasso. I was very proud. I got up and walked to the counter as he started cursing at me. I handed my waitress-with-the-long-red-hair a tensky and told her to keep the change. Then I looked into her big blue eyes and winked. She smiled, her wide mouth revealing gorgeous white teeth, the top front two with a big gap between them. I walked out onto Northern Boulevard and despite the heat of that July night, I was cool. I was Steve McQueen.

three

Most nights that summer I came home around eleven or eleven thirty. My mother would always be awake and we would watch *The Honeymooners* or *The Twilight Zone* together. The night I buried Willie's face in his triple-burger deluxe I got home earlier than usual. Mom was surprised . . . Wait . . . Hold on a second . . .

Let's stop here and go back. I'm sorry. I'm a liar. A liar and a coward.

I did none of the valiant things I described.

I did not tell Willie he ate like a cow, had shitty taste in music, and laughed like a little girl.

I did not put Willie's face into his cheeseburgers like he deserved.

I did not hand the-waitress-with-the-long-red-hair a tensky and tell her to keep the change.

I was not cool nor was I Steve McQueen.

No.

I did absolutely nothing that night. I suffered Willie's humiliation of me and the slandering of my fair maiden in silence.

I ate my cheeseburger, drank my Coke, and split

the check with Willie, and we walked back to his house like nothing had happened at all. I can't even say that I was filled with hate for the guy. Well, maybe that night I was. Maybe that night I wished the Q32 bus would squash him into a humongous pancake that I could feed to all the starving children of Biafra and Bangladesh and win the Nobel Peace Prize.

And maybe not. Maybe I just felt sad for this poor, unfortunate soul. A pathetic behemoth doomed to live out his days trapped in a mind the size of a postage stamp. No . . .

More lies. Forgive me.

Willie was not as fat as I've made him out to be. He was kind of flabby and chubby but not exactly obese.

I don't want to write about Willie anymore, thank you.

So I did get home my usual time that night after all. Just as the full moon rose into the sky over the opening credits of *The Honeymooners*. My mother always tried to be cheery when I came in and would ask if I had fun. My answer was invariably "Yes." I knew she was tortured and tormented over the breakup and the passing of my father. Watching her force herself to look like everything was fine made me sad. It also made me hate him even more. Which is a terrible way to feel about your dear old dead dad. But that's the truth. I'd yet to find any sympathy or compassion for the man.

You see, the straw that broke the marriage was my dad having an affair with a tenant of my mother's cousin. So the whole family, and many of our friends and neighbors, knew that he was fucking the young Lithuanian chick who lived in cousin Joan's basement. My mother was humiliated and her heart was broken. And it wasn't the first time, but it would be the last. Then after he died she felt even worse. I know she felt bad for me: a teenage boy without a father. But I think she felt bad for my dad too, and I think she missed him. And despite all the pain he caused us, despite all the selfish shit he indulged in, I think she blamed herself for the whole thing.

And all I did to ease her pain was spend half an hour every night watching TV with her. At the time, this felt like a big sacrifice on my part. A great Act of Charity. What a guy.

As the summer rolled on, my mother became more dependent on some kind of downer/barbiturate, most likely quaaludes. I never found them, even though I searched the house high and low. I wouldn't have taken them myself; pills weren't my thing. I just wanted to dump them into the toilet so she wouldn't eat them anymore. I always knew when she was high. She would get all glassy-eyed, smiley, and slack-jawed. She fell asleep with a lit cigarette on several occasions. I was sure she would soon burn the house down.

four

On July 31 my maternal grandfather Gus Lombard had a heart attack while driving his car somewhere in Brooklyn. My grandma Betty was also in the car. Fortunately they just rolled slowly into a few parked cars and she wasn't hurt. But her husband of forty-something years slumped dead in her lap. You can imagine the state my mother fell into after everything that had already happened.

At the funeral a black woman sang a gospel song. Her voice was powerful and moving. It shook the whole church and made everyone who was crying cry even more. She was the only black person in the building.

My cousin Nicky told me that my grandfather used to sleep with her now and then. This I found hard to accept. The notion of Grandpa Gus having sex with anyone at all was difficult for me, so the idea that he slept with this black woman was downright unfathomable. The woman was at least twenty years younger than my grandpa and for as long as I could remember, the man had nothing good to say about any black person outside of Nat King Cole and Willie Mays.

Nicky told me that the woman was a customer in my grandpa's store and that her husband had died in Vietnam. Gramps let her open an account for her groceries, which was something he very rarely did. He also allowed her to call in for her orders (another rarity) and would make her deliveries personally. Thus began a love affair that lasted seven or eight years, or so the story goes.

The truth of the romance has never been completely confirmed. But on that Astorian August morning the woman sang her guts out. She put every possible ounce of feeling into the stirring melody. She must have felt something for the man.

My mother gave her a big hug after the service. My mother gave everybody a big hug after the service. It was like she was trying to extract pieces of my grandfather's spirit out of everyone who knew him. Like if she squeezed everyone hard enough it would somehow reconstitute his being and he would rematerialize alive and well before us.

I miss him. I loved him a lot. It was already a rough summer for me but my concern for my mother outweighed my grief. She was getting high more often and I was scared she would OD and kill herself or wind up in a psych ward somewhere. For the first two weeks after my grandfather's death it looked like one or the other was inevitable.

I stayed home as much as I could without going batshit myself. She didn't want to go anywhere or do anything so I made us sandwiches for lunch every afternoon and more sandwiches for dinner every evening. I am not much of cook. The lunch sandwich would be her breakfast because she slept till two in the afternoon every day. Just in time to turn on the TV and catch her soap operas. The TV would remain on till she passed out in the wee hours. If I woke up during the night I'd turn it off, but very often it stayed on until I rose the next morning.

It was heavy and oppressive being alone with her every day. It was also hot as all fuck. The air conditioner was broken and she was way too out of it to care. She was sliding down a nasty slope of addiction and depression and there was nothing I could do about it.

At least once a day she would be sitting in front of the TV watching *General Hospital* or some shit and tears would just roll down her face. Big watery tears that left trails of dirt and makeup as they made their way south. The weird thing was that she didn't really look sad. She was blank, no expression, nothing in her face giving away any grief or pain. This unnerved me more than if she were overcome by a loud jag of sobs and crying. I wished she would moan and wail like a normal human being instead of the empty zombified shell she'd become. I was not equipped to deal with her and she'd stopped letting anyone at all, family or friend, into the house.

And then one day around the middle of August I woke up to the sound of our vacuum cleaner. It had been silent for months. My mother had gotten up early and was giving the house a thorough cleaning. She looked different that day, she was smiling at me but not in a dopey narcotic way. It was a lucid and peaceful smile. Her hair was combed and her clothes weren't wrinkled. She kissed me good morning and cooked me breakfast in a clean kitchen.

It seemed like she had picked herself up by the bootstraps, snapped out of despair, and made a decision not to let it all go down the drain. That afternoon she started packing things into suitcases and boxes. I didn't ask why. When we sat down to lunch (she made chili with Minute rice—my favorite) she told me that we were going to move into the city.

She may as well have said that we were moving to North Dakota. If you lived in Jackson Heights, Manhattan was that far away. Maybe we would go once or twice a year to see the Christmas tree or the circus. Or if my cousins came up from Florida we would go to the Empire State Building. But not much more than that. And living there . . . well, that was uncharted waters. The city was for rich people or poor people and we didn't fall into either category.

five

My grandfather had a lot more money than I'd imagined. He took numbers in his shop and made loans to his customers for decades. There were piles and piles of cash in a safe he kept in the basement of his house. The lion's share of this booty went to my mother. I think she got even more than my grandma did, but it may have been that Grandma Betty felt sorry for her and wanted to give her a chance to start a new life.

Right before Labor Day, my mother and I took a taxi to East 52nd Street in Manhattan. The block dead-ended to a high ridge with the East River and the FDR Drive flowing below. It was a very ritzy block, even I could see that and I knew jack shit about the city. There was a Rolls Royce idling near the corner on First Avenue. A chauffeur wearing a hat was sitting behind the wheel which was on the wrong side, the British side. It was the first Rolls I had ever seen in my life.

We walked up to a big brick building. A friendly doorman let us in and handed my mother an envelope that bore her name scrawled in black ink. The smiling doorman said his name was Kenny. He had a string-beany Dick Van Dyke type of frame and a very young face. His uniform was too big for his body and he looked like a kid wearing his old man's clothes.

Kenny showed us to the elevator and rambled on about the heat and the impending rain. He seemed like a good guy even if he was a bit of a blabbermouth. He left us alone at the elevator and my mother pressed 6. Inside the envelope was a key that let us into apartment 6K at the end of a long hallway.

The living room was empty and had shiny wood floors. The windows looked out onto 52nd Street. We could see part of the river and the Queens shoreline. My mother showed me the bedroom that was going to be mine.

She went to the bathroom and I stood alone in the center of the room. There were two windows that faced the back of the very wide building just south of ours. All I could see were windows, maybe a hundred of them. A big wall of eyes or one big fly eye that was trained right at me. I could see people behind some of the eyes. I could watch them go about their daily lives. It was a strange sensation and I felt like it was wrong to be watching them. But apparently they didn't care. If they wanted privacy they could pull down the shades.

I waited for my mom in the kitchen. She was in the bathroom for a long time and I started to worry. I killed time looking through the drawers and cupboards but all I found were some chopsticks. She finally came out of the bathroom and asked me what I thought of the place.

The idea of moving scared me. The rooms were big, the building in a fancy part of town; it was all too foreign. And my mother hadn't told me anything about what our life here would be like. There were too many unknowns: Where would I go to school? Was she getting a job? Was it a temporary move and we'd go back to Queens in a few months? Or did my mother meet a new guy at some point and he was the one renting the apartment for us and now she was going to open one of the closet doors and Jerry or Jim or whoever the fuck would appear and introduce himself as my new father? I was scared of all the questions and even more scared of the answers.

I opened the refrigerator, expecting it to smell bad. It didn't. I took that as an okay sign. There was nothing inside except an open can of Coke. I emptied it into the sink.

My mother asked me the same question again: "What do you think, Mitt?" She was the only person who called me that.

"It's nice" was all I could manage to say.

She sat down Indian style in the middle of the living room and asked me to sit across from her. I did and then I noticed that she was still on the pills.

"I think we owe it to ourselves. No?"

She waited for me to reply but I didn't.

"We had a rough year and I think a new beginning would do us both a world of good."

Still no answer from me.

She stared at me and smiled. She did have a lovely smile. And if a drug was responsible for it, well . . . so be it. Pills or no pills, I think she was genuinely happy that day.

As for me, I can't really say I was *unhappy*. Yes, I was afraid, but I wasn't sad. I wasn't going to miss anybody from my neighborhood. Maybe Willie a little bit. Maybe not. I wasn't so attached to anyone except my Grandma Betty and my mother assured me we would be seeing her at least once a week. I mean, we were only fifteen minutes away from Jackson Heights by taxi or train. But psychologically it was another story. For me, the East River may as well have been the Atlantic Ocean.

"When do we move in?" It was my first real question about our new life. It would also be the only one I asked that day.

"The movers are coming Friday morning. We have a lot of work to do, Mitty."

Friday. Wow. She was wasting no time.

We took the elevator back down to the lobby. A different doorman was on duty. He smiled at us as we walked toward him but his attention was immediately drawn to the entrance. A short, skinny guy dressed in all black with big dark sunglasses and very short bleached-blond hair stumbled his way inside. He had on a black leather jacket even though it was ninety degrees.

He smelled bad. Like cigarettes, booze, BO, cheap perfume, and something like kerosene or the gas from a stove with its pilot light out. I was sure the doorman was going to throw him right out. He looked like the junkies I would see hanging out by the Roosevelt Avenue subway station hustling change for a token or a shot.

But I was wrong.

The doorman motioned to my mother and me to wait a second as he graciously greeted the man in black. "Hello, sir." He smiled as he said it.

"Hey, Arthur," the guy mumbled in a low voice. No doubt he was fucked up on something. "I might be getting a package in a little bit. Send the kid right up."

"Will do, sir."

He may have been high but he certainly belonged there. The doorman actually tipped his hat as the skinny guy propelled himself through the lobby in jerky spurts. He came right toward us and my mother and I had to move quickly to get out of his way. I don't think he even knew we were there.

As he passed us I saw that the hair on the back of his head had a cross shaved into it. Not the Jesus cross but the cross the German army wore as medals. The Iron Cross. I watched as he went into the elevator, pushed a button, and then sat down on the floor Indian style, just like we had done minutes ago. He slumped his head down like he was exhausted and disappeared behind the closing door.

"So we'll see you Friday?" the doorman said to my mother.

"Yes, Friday." Mother looked at her shoes.

"Anything I can do for you, please let us know."

My mother thanked him.

"Welcome to 446 East 52nd Street!"

He held the door open and we walked out onto our new block.

six

I sat on the edge of my bed in apartment 6K. It was around dinnertime and still lots of daylight left. I could hear footsteps on the ceiling above me, voices and shouts from the sidewalk and the building across the way, helicopters chopping the sky, ambulances and police cars wailing through the street, and maybe worst of all the incessant elevator lurching through its shaft.

How could I possibly live this way? How would I find any peace? I couldn't believe how much I could hear. I thought I was used to lots of noise. Jackson Heights wasn't exactly Hicksville. It was a pretty busy place and we lived close to the main drag, but there was no comparison to East 52nd Street. I wanted to tell my mother that this couldn't work, that it was too much for me to handle and I needed to go back to Queens.

I held my tongue and we went out for dinner. We walked to the Wellington Restaurant (a diner in actuality) a few blocks away. My mother told me that I would have an interview the next morning at what she hoped would be my new school. She said it was a private school which I took to mean a religious school. This was bad news. I was not happy at the thought of Catholic nuns and priests running my life.

But I said nothing. I kept to my strict policy of not asking questions about what was happening in our lives. The only thing I asked about was the soup of the day.

It was lentil. I ordered it and it was very good. They gave us loads of free breadsticks, little packs of crackers in cellophane, and foil-wrapped pats of butter. It seemed like an extraordinary amount of food to give away. We barely made a dent in the pile even though I gorged on it before, during, and after my soup. The waiter even gave us a paper bag and insisted we take the remainder home. Besides the doormen, he was the first friend we made in the city.

When we first walked into the diner I thought he'd be mean. Busing a table with great speed, he was curt and gruff when we entered.

"Two?" he said, and jerked his head toward a small table in the corner near the bathrooms.

My mother asked if we could have a booth.

He stopped his work, looked up at us, and scratched his shoulder. "Anywhere you like." He smiled wide and made a grand, sweeping horizontal arc with his arm. The smile revealed a big gold incisor below his bushy black mustache. The tooth so big it reflected light off the overheard fluorescent, and beamed a thin blue ray right between my eyes.

He wasn't nasty at all, just busy. In time I realized that was how most of the city's people were. They seemed cold and unkind on the surface but it was simply the armor necessary to live tightly among millions. Beneath the shell you could usually find the goodness.

Right after we ordered our meals, I spotted the guy with the Iron Cross in his head. He was sitting in a booth next to a woman with long jet-black hair. She sat between him and the plate-glass window nibbling on a muffin and sipping tea. He was pressed tight against her.

He wore the exact same getup as before: black leather jacket, T-shirt, pants, and the big black sunglasses. She wore a matching pair. He had a full plate of food in front of him: a cheese omelet with bacon, fries, and well-done toast.

He didn't touch it at all.

Not a bite.

He wasn't even holding a fork. He just sat with his head erect looking straight ahead. The large glass of OJ next to his plate was full to the brim. He didn't take so much as a sip. The only time he moved was when he reached for his woman's hand. He intertwined his fingers with hers and had her hand in his lap for the remainder of the time we were there. Resting on his knee, their hands caressed each other, twisting and turning on each other, both restless and gentle. It was tender and sweet. I couldn't take my eyes off them and I didn't know why. He was certainly strange-looking and weird-acting but the way the two of them were together in the booth made me feel good. Maybe it was because they were obviously so very much in love.

When we got back to our new home I felt much better about the place. I think it was a combination of the gold-tooth waiter's hospitality and the blond guy holding his girl's hand so affectionately that calmed me down.

I sat on my brand-new bed. My mother had bought new furniture for the apartment and trashed all of our old stuff except for two end tables that once belonged to my great-grandmother. Legend has it that she brought them from Poland.

I could hear a man shouting in the street: "Back it up!! . . . Keep her coming! . . . Keep her coming!!!"

The shouts didn't bother me at all. I put my head on the pillow. The elevator was moving less frequently but there was still a lot of noise coming from the street: trucks, cars, buses, sirens, voices . . . None of it disturbed me that night.

All the sounds blended into one big hum of white noise like a steady wind or a patient tide.

I passed out cold till morning.

seven

My new school was supposed to be this very modern and progressive institution of learning. But aside from being much smaller, it's not all that different than Newtown, the big public high school I went to in Queens. The Hobart School is in an old redbrick building on East 63rd Street in Manhattan. It's philosophy is to develop intellectual freedom, creativity, and inquisitiveness in its students and to instill a sense of compassion and respect for oneself, one's peers, and one's society.

Or something like that.

Their cutting-edge educational strategy was to coordinate the things we were learning in all of our classes and keep the themes consistent across all subjects. I thought the approach to be complete bullshit and the common course threads they prided themselves on had to be stretched real thin in order to appear synchronized and harmonious.

For instance, at the start of our junior year we focused on the Louisiana Purchase in American history; in math we dabbled in a very rudimentary overview of political economics; in English we studied the effects of colonization on language, or was it the effects of language on colonization? And in science we studied the interior waterways of the United States, particularly the Mississippi River. Music class was all about the Delta blues even though that particular form of music came about 120 years after the Purchase.

What invariably happened was that one or two of the classes would exhaust the current topic before the others. This would initiate a chain reaction/domino effect that would undermine the precious syncopation that Hobart held so dear.

So by December it was John Brown and the abolitionists, *The Sound and the Fury* (okay, I guess), an introduction to trigonometric functions (you're starting to lose me), and oil extraction in Saudi Arabia (what the fuck??). In music it was *West Side Story* because we were supposed to be reading *Romeo and Juliet* in English class—but our study of *The Scarlet Letter* took longer than expected and cut into the time originally allotted to Faulkner.

Socially, in many ways it was just a smaller version of the same old shit. You could separate all the kids into the same little boxes you'd find anyplace else: jocks, nerds, druggies, brainiacs, and sluts. The boundaries of these personality types were a little blurry at Hobart, though. There was more overlapping between species and more fluidity in the gray-zone kids who drifted between categories.

What Hobart did lack were the Cro-Magnons: the psychotically deranged violent types who stalked the halls of Newtown High. For this I was grateful; there was no love lost leaving that lot behind.

The biggest demarcation at Hobart, however, was economic, the Great Divide separating the scholarship kids (who needed to show financial hardship and a modicum of academic merit) from the ones whose parents paid the sticker price (and had to prove even less scholastic ability).

Naturally, this system separated the school into the haves and the have-nots. The favorite sport of the haves was exposing the have-nots and making certain they understood that theirs was a lower place in this tiny galaxy and, by natural extension, society at large.

Some scholarship kids were easier to spot than others. Skin color being the most obvious giveaway (the haves were often bred on prejudice for generations), and clothes a close second. Some of the scholarship kids were dirt poor, lived in the crumbling slums of the South Bronx and Bed-Stuy, and often had to wear the same clothes for two or more consecutive days. The repetition being duly noted by those who wielded the power of popularity and means.

Reconnaissance and intelligence were the other methods used to ferret out and denounce the underprivileged. A few of the haves had parents on the board of the school. Some of these noble altruists were bigger assholes than their kids and they liberally leaked information on who paid and who didn't.

I was suspected of "being on the tit." I kid you not, that's what getting a free ride was called. The endowed beneficiaries being "Tittysuckers" and often just the diminutive "Suckers." The most prevalent name for Hobart's poor and indigent was the even more abbreviated "Suck," as in, "I think the new kid's a Suck." This novel transposition of verb into noun a testament to the linguistic proficiency of our ruling class.

I dressed more like a Suck than a rich kid, which I wasn't, even though we paid. I didn't like a lot of the new clothes my mother bought me before school and I hadn't grown much over the summer so I stuck with my Wranglers and T-shirts. I was called a Suck to my face by two athletic seniors who punted a stack of books out of my hands. You see, the white Sucks were more likely to be confronted physically than the black or Puerto Rican Sucks; racist urban paranoia instilled a fear of blades and jailbird siblings into our future titans of industry and stewards (and stewardesses) of culture.

The homecoming theme that autumn was "The Best Days of Our Lives." But on the glittery blue-and-gold banner they hung over the gym's big double doors, the word *Lives* appeared as *Live's*.

Nobody bothered to change it.

eight

I noticed her on my very first day of school but it wasn't until a few weeks had passed that I found the courage to speak to her.

"You dropped your pencil."

That was it. The sentence fell from my mouth and tumbled into the abyss. The four separate words slurred into one unintelligible sound. At least that's how I remember it.

By the time this magical pencil had fallen, I had imagined all kinds of scenarios that would crack the glacier that loomed between knowing her and being a mere stranger.

"You dropped your pencil."

It's strange how things that unfold into such monumental events begin with such tiny, mundane, and ordinary moments.

"Oh . . . thank you." She smiled. It was warm and sincere, like her eyes as they focused on me and the tone and timbre of her words.

She looked down at the pencil and paused for a long second. I was paralyzed and failed to realize that she was politely (without a trace of presumption) offering me an opportunity to be chivalrous and pick it up. I was clueless and missed my cue. I just stood there timid and unsure.

I watched as she started to bend at the waist. A black shirt strained to stay tucked into a black skirt, but a small field of white flesh surrendered on the left flank. My brain reengaged itself and responded to the stimulus. Moving faster than I ever thought possible, I swooped down and scooped up her number 2 Ticonderoga. It was new: fresh-honed and stiletto sharp.

I handed it over. Standing closer to her than ever before, I was enveloped by an invisible fog, a cloud of sweet smoke and flowers. Essential oils of rose and lilac, I would later learn. It intoxicated me, made me high. I lost my bearings and my breath.

I knew her name was Veronica only because I'd heard Ms. Baker call out to her as she left the art studio one day. We had no classes together that semester, but I would see her in the halls between periods two and three and later between fifth and sixth. I knew nothing else about her.

"Who do you have for science?"

I have no recollection of saying this but Veronica later swore that I did as I gave her the pencil. I cringed when she first told me, but it doesn't really shock me that I'd say something so idiotic at such a critical moment. No surprise at all. It's a particular skill I have.

Veronica was Nica if you knew her well, but never Ronnie. Ronnie was too casual, too common, and too male for such a perfect specimen of human female. She was a beauty and a genius. She was open and innocent. Yet worldly and wise beyond her years.

She was also a Suck.

But she was one of the few, perhaps the only, Suck who hid her true identity from the population at large. This was a tribute to her intelligence and resourcefulness. Yet it required her to keep a distance from her classmates and create a persona of aloofness and eccentricity. Black clothes, eyeliner, fingernails, and hair. Clove cigarettes. Quiet, imperious, haughty, and disaffected. Nietzsche, Plath, and Yoko Ono. No interest in the school's social scene or strata. No policy with the Hobart boys. No gossiping with the girls. A loner.

And the character she created had the desired effect: she gave off no Suck vibration and she was rumored to be very, very rich. But as compensation for her nonconformity she was branded a slut and a whore, a VD-ridden nympho who'd had an abortion. Maybe two.

Veronica was an autodidact (her word, not mine)

who taught herself German and Italian over two consecutive summers after the sixth and seventh grades. This was in addition to fluency in Romanian, French, and English. She had aced the Hobart entrance exam with a perfect score. The first in the school's history.

Her fingers were always stained with violet ink and she was endlessly filling up pages of notebooks during, in between, and after classes. She was a writer and said so. Not "one day I hope to be a writer." But was in fact at work on her second novel. She had read in an interview with Norman Mailer or Gore Vidal or someone like that that one's first novel should be put in a drawer until the second novel was finished. True to this axiom, she stowed her debut in a box under her bed as she toiled away on volume two.

"Never give them any ammunition."

This was the reasoning behind keeping herself a mystery to our fellow students.

"Subvert them from within their own rank and file."

Brave words from a courageous young woman, but deep down I think she was embarrassed about being poor. I think it made her feel ashamed.

nine

My mother thought it would be a good idea if I got a part-time job. I agreed with her. I liked to work and I liked having my own money. It made me feel mature and manly. When I was fourteen I got a job stocking shelves in a small hardware store not far from our house in Jackson Heights. The store was called Halloran's Hardware but it was owned by a Jewish man named Lippman.

Mr. Lippman was very old by the time I started to work for him. I gathered through his stories and reminiscences that he probably bought the business sometime before World War II.

Mr. Lippman liked me a lot. The day I started my second week of work he bought us egg rolls, fried rice, and steak kew from Lum's Chinese restaurant. It became a weekly ritual. We would eat together at the counter and he would talk about the history of the neighborhood and how sad it was that things were changing so quickly and that soon we would all be speaking Spanish. I wasn't so aware of the rapid metamorphosis that was happening around us but it made Mr. Lippman sad.

Mr. Lippman lived with his wife above the store. She had become sickly in recent years, so every few hours he would go upstairs and check on his beloved Zohra, leaving me alone behind the register. He trusted me that much. And in return, I stole from the man.

I justified the thievery by convincing myself that I wasn't being paid enough. But this didn't help. I still felt horrible doing it, though not horrible enough to stop.

I never got caught.

It was a very simple scheme: when a customer would pay for something small like a box of nails or a bottle of glue, I would "accidentally" push a pen off the counter so it fell near the customer's feet. As the person bent to pick it up, I would hit *No Sale* and open the register without entering the price of the item. By the time the customer stood back up I would be handing him the change and bagging his order.

My fear was that Mr. Lippman would notice a discrepancy between inventory and sales, but that never happened. What did happen is that I put a few extra bucks in my pocket and felt like a royal piece of shit. And after each heist, I vowed to never do it again. But I did it many times.

The worst was always when he came back downstairs from god knows what kind of miserable scenario with his invalid wife.

"No fires or tornadoes?"

This was always the first thing he would say upon his return and he would crack a little grin. I couldn't face him as I answered, "No." I couldn't bring myself to return the grin.

They say the first time you commit a crime is the hardest and that the subsequent crimes become easier and easier. You become immune and hardened to the transgression and whatever suffering is inflicted on the victim. This was not the case for me. I felt worse and worse each time I did it. And the question "No fires or tornadoes?" became more and more unbearable.

When Mr. Lippman's wife died he closed the store, ending my life of crime and relieving me of the shame of facing his bushy gray mustache, his heavy shoes, his kind and trusting nature, his shuffling steps on the weary stairs.

I promised myself things would be different now that I was older and had started my life over in a new city (or borough, to be precise). I vowed to never steal again as I walked down the street to the Wellington, my favorite place in the neighborhood so far. I asked the woman behind the register if they were hiring. She stared at me while poking at her teeth with a toothpick.

"What do you do?" she asked.

I didn't know quite how to answer so I just said: "I'm flexible."

"Well, we don't need no acrobats." I didn't realize she was making a joke and thought she had somehow misunderstood me. But as I stammered and searched for a reply, she yelled toward the kitchen: "Hey, Ciro, do we still need another delivery guy?"

The owner, a squat man who always looked as if he had just received some sort of bad news, came through the swinging doors wiping his hands on his apron. His eyes were immediately upon me, sizing me up and down. Then he jutted his chin in my direction and said with a European accent: "Do you have any experience?"

"Yes."

I guess he believed me because his next question was: "Do you go to school? . . . Where do you go to school?"

"Hobart."

"Hunter?"

Hunter was a college a few blocks up the road. I was confused. There was no way I could pass for a college student at that point in time and he didn't look like he was teasing me. So I told him the truth: "It's a private high school."

"Oh yes, that's a very good school . . . you must be a very smart boy." He seemed genuinely impressed. If only he could see some of the morons who were my classmates. "When can you work?"

"Weekends and after school . . ."

"Can you work after school and do all the homework?"

"I don't get much homework." That was the truth. We didn't get much and you had to be really dumb not to do well. (Plus, the grades were inflated to make the school look better than it really was, but that's another story.)

"Your father, he lets you work?" said Ciro.

"My father's in California. I live with my mother. It was her idea that I get a job." I wasn't telling many people the truth about my father at that point.

"*California dreamer . . . and such a winner say . . .*" Ciro raised an arm in victory as he sang the chorus. "You know the song?"

I nodded.

"I want to go to California. If I live in California maybe I have ten restaurants by now."

The woman behind the register who hadn't seemed to be paying attention to us rolled her eyes and muttered a derisive "Hmmmph."

Ciro turned to her, the news he wore on his face going from bad to worse. "You don't think so but then you complain! Lots of complain, complain, complain!"

She bore no resemblance to him so I assumed they were married.

"Who complains? I'm too busy to complain!"

Ciro dismissed this last comment with a wave and turned back to me. He agreed to hire me on a trial basis. The trial being that if he didn't like the way I worked, he would fire me. Made sense to me.

I was to start that Saturday at seven in the morning. He told me that weekends were busy with breakfast deliveries and the tips were pretty good because it was working people enjoying their days off after payday. Weekend customers were in better moods than weekday customers, and they tipped better. The weekend shifts were eight hours each, seven am till three in the afternoon. He also offered me three weekday shifts after school from four till eight in the evening. I could have a free meal for every shift I worked—any sandwich, an omelet, a hamburger, eggs, pancakes, or waffles. I thought this was a very fair arrangement and was eager to get to work. On this we shook hands and he gave me a Coke to go.

ten

Right away, I loved my job. The people I delivered food to fascinated me; their personalities, their families, their lovers, their pets . . . every customer was different. Some wouldn't allow you so much as a glimpse inside their apartment, preferring to a make the transaction in the hallway, lobby, even the street. But more often I'd be invited into the apartment and would stand in the doorway, the kitchen, or the living room while my customer went searching for cash.

Ciro was right: the weekend customers and the weekday customers were a different species. Week-enders were likely to be family people sleeping in on Saturday or Sunday; lots of coffee, pancakes, waffles, muffins, bacon, hot chocolate, and donuts for the kids. They were in good spirits, rarely in a hurry, and yes, they tipped well. Weekdays, at least the hours I worked, were mostly single people or couples without kids; soups, burgers, chili, goulash if we had it, London broil, flounder, and salmon. These weekday folks tended to be lonelier and wanted to talk a bit and ask me questions. This could easily cross the line into creep territory, as it did with Mr. Gebberts of 301 East 66th Street, apartment 6D. The D for deranged, demented, and degenerate.

Mr. Gebberts lived in a small and sparse flat that was cleaner than any home or institution I'd ever been in. It smelled of bleach, like some kind of industrial cleaning fluid. There was a strange sterility to both the place and the man. Something was off. Like the hypercleanliness was an effort to compensate for things twisted, filthy, and perhaps diabolic.

When I would deliver his food (always a BLT on toast, extra mayo, but all the mayo on the side and a Coke with no ice and two lemons), he would have me stand on paper towels which he would spread into a large rectangle by the door. This was a tedious ritual that always took far longer than it should have. The unrolling of the paper, the slow tearing along the perforations, the exact parallels and perpendiculars he sought as he put the pieces of Bounty in place.

"If you want to come in and sit down you have to take your shoes off."

I didn't want to come in. I didn't want to sit down. And I definitely wasn't taking anything off.

Gebberts was well into his sixties but his hair, eyebrows, and mustache were all dyed way too black. His face was pink and shiny, greasy shiny, and his head was tilted strangely off-axis. He always wore these tight red-and-black exercise-type clothes. His fingernails were as shiny as his face and were lacquered to a mirror glaze. He wore buckets of cologne—clouds of it fogged the room and I would smell like him for hours after leaving his pad. It revolted me. *He* revolted me. I wouldn't have been surprised if there was some twelve-year-old girl gagged and hog-tied in a spotless bedroom closet.

The man never knew where his wallet was despite the lack of clutter in the antiseptic apartment he called home. It always took like fifteen minutes of shuffling around, clearing his throat every five seconds, disappearing and reappearing in and out of the few rooms he occupied. He would attempt conversation while the search was on:

"Are you Ciro's son?" I don't know how many times he asked me this.

"No."

"Well, you must be a relation. I can see the resemblance."

I looked nothing like the man.

"I've known Ciro for fifteen years. Did he tell you that?"

Yes, of course, we have nothing better to do down at the diner than discuss you, our dear Mr. Gebberts.

"I was his first customer when he took over from Mr. Edelman."

Everybody claimed to be Ciro's first customer.

"We're not related. I just work for him."

"Which parish do you belong to?"

What? Was this guy fucking serious?

"I don't belong to any."

"No? Are you new to the neighborhood?"

"We just moved here from Queens."

"A Queens boy! You must be a Met fan like me. I'm obsessed with them! Haven't missed a televised game in over ten years."

"I like the Yankees," I lied; the notion of having anything in common with this deviant was unbearable.

"A Queens boy who likes the Yankees? What's wrong with you?"

What's wrong with *me*?

"My father liked the Yankees." Another lie. My father was a Dodger fan before, during, and after the defection. Maybe that's what lured him to California and his fiery demise.

"Well, I won't hold it against you."

Please do. Hold it against me. That was the point of the lies.

"Where do you go to school?"

"Hobart."

"Very chic." He raised his eyebrows to sharp

jack-o'-lantern points. "Do you have a girlfriend?" He handed me the cash finally.

"No," I mumbled as I started making change.

"Keep it." A dime. A thin lousy dime, but from the way he said it, you'd think he was sponsoring my college fund. I didn't say thank you. I just turned, stepped off the paper towel island, and went out the door.

"Stop by for coffee when you feel like it."

I wouldn't stop by for coffee if the apocalypse was imminent and his apartment was the only safe haven in the galaxy. I shut the door behind me and was at the elevator when he followed me into the hallway.

"Let's go Mets!"

What a fucking freak.

Walking back to the diner after my first Gebberts encounter, I toyed with the idea that the guy was in fact a ghost and that in reality I had been standing in an empty, abandoned apartment. Perhaps the limboed spirit of Gebberts had created the illusion that I was interacting with a living, breathing human in an actual home. Maybe the sanitary extremis was needed to combat the constant excretion of unholy astral ectoplasm bubbling and erupting out of various ghastly orifices.

I was terrified every time his name appeared on

a delivery ticket. And to this day my ghost theory remains a legitimate possibility. Perhaps Gebberts the Cleanly Ghost will forever haunt 301 East 66th Street, eternally ordering BLT on toast, looking at some hapless delivery boy from a sidelong, stiff-necked angle that made his head appear abnormally small.

 . . . *Let's go Mets!*

eleven

Ciro asked me to work until midnight one Saturday evening. I had to ask permission from my mother. She said it was okay but that she wanted to pick me up when my shift was finished. I understood her concern but it made no sense because I already spent hours up until midnight walking all over the East Side, going in and out of buildings and strangers' apartments.

At around eleven that night Lorenzo, the weekend manager, gave me a ticket for the building I lived in. The delivery was for apartment 8A, which I figured was one of the penthouses. The name on the order was *Jones*, which didn't ring any bells. It was a weird order: two large OJs, two strawberry milkshakes, two double orders of bacon (a total of four orders), and *lots of pickles*.

Strange, but far from the strangest for sure. That dubious honor went to Miss A. Lundgren, a 400-pound woman who lived on East 68th Street. Miss Lundgren, dubbed "Circus Circus" by Ciro, had a standing order every Saturday and Sunday morning. At nine thirty a.m. she expected to be delivered to her door: half a dozen eggs sunny-side up, twelve sausage links, eight slices of toast with ten small packets of grape jelly, a triple order of home fries, and three large chocolate milks. Included as a courtesy in one of the bags was a full-size glass bottle of Heinz ketchup. The order stood for two years straight until one Saturday she didn't answer the door and was never heard from again.

When I got to my building with 8A's order in hand, the new doorman Jeff was on duty. I liked Jeff a lot. He reminded me of a character in an old Western who would play a sheriff or a train conductor. He was a tall, sturdy, healthy-looking guy. A Midwestern oh-my-gosh type with neatly trimmed hair and respectful, old-fashioned manners. He didn't seem to belong in New York City at all.

But Jeff was far from straitlaced. He had a fetishistic obsession with ballerinas and would often hang around the entrance to the ballet school at Lincoln Center. He would lean against the building and pretend to read the paper but he'd really be watching the young dancers come and go from their classes. He wasn't at all shy about sharing any of this with me and spoke of his fixation very casually. As if it was something that any normal American male would appreciate.

The girls who took classes there were young: from high school age down to like ten years old. Jeff would get this devilish twinkle in his eye when he described these aspiring dancers "in their little pink leotards and soft satin shoes . . . so small and petite." He tended to like the girls on the older edge of the spectrum, thank god, and especially got off watching them smoke cigarettes and curse. Jeff claimed that ballerinas had some of the filthiest mouths anywhere.

I didn't feel the need to be announced, so I didn't tell Jeff where I was going. I was sure they were expecting me. The door to apartment 8A was about halfway open and I could see into the main room. There was a low wooden table in the middle of the space and not much else in terms of furniture. A reel-to-reel tape recorder sat on top of the table and its wheels were spinning. There were cabinet speakers on both sides of the table, their innards pumping out a loud, distorted drone which I guessed was most likely from an electric guitar—a fact deduced from the sight of two electric guitars that leaned against a wall. One guitar was red, the other black. The red one had holes in it, the black one did not. They looked like a happy couple.

There were lots of books piled on top of lots of big cardboard boxes bearing the name and logo of RCA electronics. Most of the books were paperbacks and were stacked outrageously high into towers that teetered on the verge of collapse. Tons of notebooks and yellow legal pads, scribbled-up sheets of paper, pens and pencils. Some of the cardboard crates had rows of empty bottles sitting on top, neatly arranged like chess pieces and segregated into wine, beer, and liquor sections.

Lo and behold. It was him. The blond man with the Iron Crossed head was crouching beside the low table, manning the tape deck.

Was he Jones?

His lady sat Indian style on an Oriental-looking cushion, her back to the door. I stood at the threshold holding their food. I could feel the heat slowly waning from the bacon as I waited for someone to notice me. For some reason I didn't feel right knocking or clearing my throat or saying anything at all. I just continued to watch and wait.

There was no rug on the hardwood floor. I thought it looked like a cold surface to sit on even with a cushion. But the pair didn't seem to mind. He hit a knob on the deck and the reels stopped spinning. The speakers went quiet. He hit another knob and the tape spun the opposite way. He replayed the droning guitar.

"That part, right there, that's the part I'm talking about. Do you hear it?" He jotted something onto a coffee-stained legal pad. A cigarette burned in an ashtray on top of the same yellow page.

"Yes, I hear it." Her voice was quiet and I couldn't tell if she had an accent or not.

"That's what I'm trying to do. That's what the whole shot is about. It's all there in that one riff."

"You've done it." She spoke soft and kind.

"Now what? . . . Now what, baby?" He said this as if he really wanted an answer from her, but this was definitely not the case.

"That's always the question, isn't it?" She did have an accent. Maybe Spanish or Portuguese.

He chuckled with a childlike pitch that surprised me. It took some of the edge off his menacing aura. Then, as his laughter subsided, he turned his head in my direction. "Hello." He said it flatly but his eyes had the intensity of a brain surgeon staring down the tumor in a young boy's head. "What are you, like fourteen? Jesus Christ! Tell Fernando he can't send kids to my place! What, is he trying to get me fucking arrested?!"

He scared me. I didn't know what the hell he was talking about or who Fernando was. I wanted to tell him that I lived downstairs but I thought that would confuse him even more so I just held up the bags of food.

"I have your delivery." When I spoke, the woman

turned her head. She was exotic-looking with high cheekbones and dark eyes. Mexican or Indian or maybe from Spain. She glanced at me and then quickly looked down.

"What?!" He shouted it like he was expecting some kind violence to happen.

"He's from the diner, Lou," she said.

"Oh . . . oh yeah." He relaxed a little. "Where's the old man? Did you mug him or something?"

"No, ummm. I just started working there a few weeks ago . . . and I . . ."

"I'm kidding, man." He chuckled again. "What's the matter? Can't you take a joke? How much I owe you?"

"Seven fifty-five."

The moaning feedback echoed from the speakers. He stood up and started searching his pockets. I smelled the kerosene on him again. She looked back up at me. Her eyes were gentle but I was uncomfortable. I felt like she was waiting for me to do something or for something to happen. I didn't know what that was, but I had a strong feeling that I had forgotten to do it or didn't know how. I became very confused and disoriented.

Whatever specific energetic vibration they gave off as individuals was new to me—that I understood. But as a couple the voltage was magnified and amplified: a white-hot current looping between transponder towers. My heart began to race, I was nauseous and sweating. Maybe it wasn't them, maybe it was the recording that upset my equilibrium. Everything became alien and dangerous. My knees started shaking. I wanted to run but my legs felt stiff and heavy.

I made a big effort to focus on the reason I was there: the transaction of food for money. He was rifling through his pockets with a jittery manic urgency, like there were a hundred pockets in his pants and one of them held a ticking bomb. My mouth went dry and my tongue was swollen; I didn't think I was going to make it.

After searching each pocket at least ten times, he gave up and turned to the woman. "Where's my money, honey?"

"Check your shoe, Lou."

Lou.

Lou laughed, then looked at me: "Hop on the bus, Gus." He turned off the music.

I regained my faculties, my heart slowed down, I stopped sweating, the nausea went away. The woman smiled sweetly at me. Lou's eyes softened and he went on reciting rhymes.

"Just drop off the key, Lee. And put your hand on my knee." He walked to a corner of the room and reached into an ankle-high black leather boot with a high heel. From its depths he recovered a neatly folded banknote and handed it to me. It was a hundred-dollar bill. "Here you go, sport."

"I'm sorry, sir . . . but I don't have enough change for that."

"Well go get it."

"Okay, I'll be right back." I handed over his order and turned to leave.

"Where do you think you're going?"

I turned back around to face him. "I'm going to get some change for you."

He snatched the hundred out of my hand and gave me back the food. His eyes got big, hard, and piercing again. His head twitched like a rooster's. "The fuck you think, I'm stupid? You think I'd actually fall for that shit? I invented that fucking scam back in Brooklyn, you little prick! Get the fuck out of my house!!"

His arms were moving fast and randomly, waving in my face as he spoke. It looked like he had four of them from my perspective. I was frightened more for him than for me and I was pretty scared. He seemed like he was about to croak from a heart attack, stroke, or conniption fit. I apologized but my words had no effect.

"Maybe you and the old man are in cahoots and

this whole thing is a setup. Send him over and I'll stab the fucker with a bread knife!!"

"It's not a setup, I promise." I didn't recognize my own voice as it came out of my mouth. "I'll go to the diner and get your change, sir. You hold onto your money. I'm very, very sorry." I started out the door but a claw gripped my shoulder hard.

"No, no, no . . . too late . . . too late for that . . . we have to settle this once and for all, we're gonna get your boss on the phone. We're gonna make sure all your bullshit checks out 'cause right now I don't know who the fuck I got in my house and I got a woman to protect, motherfucker . . . Rachel, call the restaurant."

Rachel.

His nails dug into my skin and I pulled away as gently as I could. He twisted the fabric of my jacket to grab me tighter.

"You ain't goin' nowhere, you punk. I should call my friends down the fucking—"

"Baby . . ." Rachel interrupted his rant. "He's just a kid. Let him go and get change. He brought our food, let him get change and then we'll pay him." She shook her head and looked at me. I sensed she was trying to communicate that everything was cool and not to take him so seriously.

He grabbed the bag out of my hand and started

to pull all the items out one by one. "What did we order, hon? Who ordered all this bacon?"

"We did, Lou."

"Pink milkshakes . . . oh yeah. Okay, okay, okay. Looks like you got it right, kid." He turned to Rachel. "You trust him, hon?"

"Yes, I do. I trust him."

Lou sized me up for a few long seconds. "Rachel is extremely intuitive and possesses psychic ability. I call her the Panamanian Shaman. She has uncanny insight into the human mind and motivation. Don't ruin it for me, okay?"

I wasn't sure what he meant by that question but I assured him I wouldn't ruin it and that I would be right back with the correct change. Yet before I was able to turn around and go, he lunged at me. His move was quick and sudden. I raised my hands and closed my eyes, expecting to be thrown against the wall or to the floor. But he just put his arms around me and hugged. His body was stiff and tense, his ropy muscles flexed. But it wasn't a sleazy ulterior-motive thing or anything like that. It seemed like sincere affection and an apology. It touched me as much as it surprised me. And it was over as abruptly as it began. He kept his hands on my shoulders as he pulled away.

"What was your name again, kid?"

I hadn't mentioned my name. Or had I? I'd lost track of what was said and done and how much time had elapsed since I got there. It could have been two minutes or an hour; my perception of time had been debilitated. And the hug had really thrown me for a loop.

"Matthew." I had to think about it for a second.

"Okay, Matt. Can I call you Matt? See you in a few minutes." He released his hands from my shoulders; I walked out the door.

"Hey, Matt!" I looked back at him and he was holding the hundred-dollar bill between his index and middle fingers. "Aren't you forgetting something?" He strode to me and shoved the bill into my hand.

"Thanks, Matthew," Rachel said from the cushion. She was turned about three-quarters toward me and smiling beatific at Lou, then at me. The fluorescent light coming from the kitchen hit the side of her face like a slash of daytime. It revealed a subtle stubble of beard struggling to surface through the thick layer of makeup on her face.

"See you in a bit, Matty me boy," Lou said as he closed the door politely in my face.

I walked down the corridor as the guitars began screaming once again.

twelve

I returned to apartment 8A out of breath from running to and from the diner. I was only gone about fifteen minutes but the atmosphere had totally changed. It was quiet and calm.

Lou was happy to see me but I think he forgot my name. He kept calling me Jack. Rachel was still on the cushion but now she had a box of beads open in her lap and sipped on an OJ. She was sorting through and separating the various colors and sizes. I gave Lou his change and he gave me a ten-dollar tip. It was the biggest tip I would ever get as a delivery boy.

He invited me to sit and offered me one of the strawberry shakes. I sat on the floor across the table from him and told him I could only stay for a minute.

"Where you from, Jack?" He chomped on some bacon.

"Queens, but now we live here."

"Whereabouts?"

"Here, downstairs . . . on the sixth floor."

"What?"

My answer confused him as I predicted. He couldn't connect me working at the diner with me living two floors beneath him. Before I could elaborate, he lit a cigarette and changed the subject.

"Rachel had a good feeling about you and I trust her instincts implicitly. Do you believe in past lives?"

"I never really thought about it." That was the truth, I hadn't up until that point.

"The Hindus, the Buddhists, the Hare Krishnas, they all believe in the concept of reincarnation. They think we've had many lives before this one and will have many more after this, and everybody always thinks they were a king or a pharaoh but they could have just as easily been an insect or a three-legged dog or a slitherer with suction cups. Right, hon?" He stopped talking, looked at her, and waited.

She started to unspool some wire and without looking up began talking: "You are reborn according to the karma you create and bring with you from one life to the next, but whatever your past life may have been, it bares little resemblance to who you are today because what we consider ourselves to be, the 'me' that we identify so strongly with, is merely a collection of patterns, habits, thoughts, ideas, impressions, and histories that have been cobbled together from various causes and conditions that arose due to prior karma; the self is an illusion, as empty as a rainbow. What does get reincarnated is purely an impartial, impersonal, and wholly energetic field that has become imbued with a positivity and/or negativity outside of any identifiable qualities of self."

The above being my best attempt at recreating her theory of karma and rebirth, as heard by me on several subsequent occasions, but always in the same torrent of words and ideas. She looked up at Lou when she finished speaking, then at me briefly, then back down at her wire and beads.

"She's fucking brilliant, no?" Lou shook his head in admiration.

I nodded and sucked down some shake. I had to get back to the diner. My mother was coming to pick me up in fifteen minutes, which was an absurdity in itself since I was already home, but I didn't want to have to explain everything to her. I felt it best to keep my new friends a secret.

"Come back and see us soon, Jack." Lou gave me a strange-looking paperback by someone named Lobsang Rampa along with another big hug.

"You're welcome anytime," Rachel said as she strung up some beads.

"Do you take dictation?" Lou asked as he escorted me out the door.

I surprised myself by saying yes.

"Come by Friday afternoon, I could use the

help." He slammed the door without waiting for my response. Then I heard a loud crash from inside his apartment, something big and heavy must have fallen to the floor.

I stopped and listened, debating whether I should check it out or not. It was still and quiet again; too quiet. I started to walk back to the door when the silence was broken by Lou, who laughed long and loud. Eleven forty-five and all was well.

thirteen

Veronica told me she was a witch right after the Christmas break was over. She claimed to be the current heiress to a magical (or *magickal* as she preferred to spell it) lineage passed from mother to daughter over twenty-one generations. A line unbroken for over five hundred years. She said her family traced its roots to the Carpathian region of Romania and that her mother's ancestors arrived in America over two hundred years ago.

I found it hard to swallow that a succession of women gave birth to baby girls without fail for hundreds of years. I suppose stranger things have happened on this planet, and when you are operating in the occult world the unpredictable becomes more likely—maybe—if you believe in that stuff.

Perhaps there were times when only a male was born and they had to fudge the records and the wife of the witch's son would become the inheritor of the "art," as Veronica called it. I told her this theory of mine and it pissed her off.

She explained that her great-great-great-great-

(etc.)-grandmother had sworn an oath and with her last breath pledged a curse before she was burned at the stake in Romania. Having had the prescience to send her only daughter to France before her arrest, Great-Grandma the Witch made a dying promise that this female line would last for a thousand years to "right the wrongs of her murderers and punish them and their progeny for centuries." As Veronica told me this, she stared into my eyes for a long time without blinking.

I'd like to believe the purpose of her deep gaze was to emphasize the gravity of the story rather than an intimidation tactic, but I must admit that a chill ran through me. I sensed a queer sort of power emanating from her. I never felt it from her again and she never looked at me in quite the same way, but on that very gray January afternoon, sitting on a bench with our backs to Central Park . . . I believed she was a witch indeed.

I asked her what kind of things she did with her witchcraft powers.

"We call it *art*, not *power*. And all I can say about it is that I am able to assert my will in a certain way that can have a subtle influence over the way events unfold."

"Can you give me an example?"

"No. I don't know you well enough. I've probably

told too much already . . . But you have nothing to worry about. You're my friend, so don't be scared or anything."

"I'm not scared at all." That was not entirely true.

"Good," she said as she took my hand in hers for the first time.

We stared straight out toward Fifth Avenue and watched the cars, buses, and taxis flow downtown. She didn't look at me for a long time.

As I held onto her hand, I felt certain that she was telling the truth and I never needed to worry about her harming me. Anything she did to me that seemed challenging or confrontational was only to test me and train me into being more like she was: confident, strong, and fearless. All things that I was not. She took this on as a mission or duty. She said that the city was going to eat me alive if I didn't wise up, that Jackson Heights and Manhattan were as far apart as Bumfuck and Hollywood. I agreed.

When I walked her to the subway later that afternoon, she told me that she had turned her first trick right around this time last year.

fourteen

The dictation session never happened.

I didn't make it to Lou's apartment for several weeks after that first delivery. He had gone to Europe to play some concerts, I was told by Kenny the doorman:

"Mr. ____ is quite the character, isn't he?"

Mr. ____. He wasn't Jones. Now I put it all together and I realized who he was. I did not know much about his music, except for the chorus of the one song, but I knew his name.

I ran into him in the lobby a few days after he returned. He was happy to see me and brought up the dictation again and I agreed to stop by the next afternoon.

I arrived about four o'clock. The door was open a crack so I knocked on the jamb.

"Come on in!" he shouted from inside.

There was a window wide open and it was cold in the apartment. The place looked like I had never left it except Rachel wasn't there and Lou was talking quietly into a red telephone on the kitchen counter.

He held up a finger signaling he'd be right with me. I stood awkwardly in the living area until he finished his call.

When Lou hung up, he invited me to sit on the floor and then offered me a Hershey's bar. "If you don't want it, save it for later."

I put it in my jacket pocket. He dropped a yellow legal pad and a pen onto the floor next to me. He explained that Rachel had gone up to the Bronx to visit her mother: "A mother and her daughter, you know . . . they can't be apart for too long. It's a deep bond."

I gripped the pen and was waiting for him to start dictating. He explained that he was working on a biography of one of the saints, I don't remember which one, though it was not a factual, historical biography but more like an imagined interpretation of this holy man's life. He explained further that it was to be the book or libretto of an opera that he was also writing the music for.

"Okay, okay, okay . . . do you have a cigarette? . . . No, you don't smoke . . . Good, don't . . . it's a filthy habit." He found his pack under a leather jacket that was tossed over a cardboard RCA-marked box. "So we were just in Amsterdam, don't write this down . . . and you know in Amsterdam—" The phone's ringer interrupted him. "Be right with you, pal."

He stayed on the phone for over an hour. I

couldn't hear what he was saying because he was speaking in hushed, low tones. In the meantime, I ate the Hershey's bar and read from a book of short stories on one of his stacks. It was about an Englishman who gets captured by some North African tribespeople who cut out his tongue and keep him chained up. They force him to be the jester in the court of the bedouin king. It was a horrifying story and the image of the man dressed in cut-up cans of Coca-Cola stayed in my mind for weeks.

When Lou finally got off the phone he acted as if the call had taken no more than a minute. "Okay, okay, okay . . . you got the pad? Good . . . Oh, wait, you know what's funny? Don't write this down . . . I was walking by my old house on the Bowery and I see this old man sitting against a wall—" The phone rang again and he dashed to the kitchen. This time he spoke for only about forty minutes or so.

I picked up another book, this one about a man who was in love with a beautiful Mexican woman with a serious addiction to heroin. This story was not nearly as disturbing as the first one I'd read. I got through about twenty-five pages when Lou came back.

"You can borrow any of those, by the way . . . Okay, okay, okay . . . Act one, scene one . . . Wait, I didn't finish my story . . . don't write this down . . . So

I'm down the Bowery and I see this old guy sitting against a wall near my old house, he looks kind of familiar but he's a bum, you know, a piss-in-the-pants drunk, but I know I've seen his face before . . . and he's looking at me and he goes, *What are you looking at, faggot?* I'm about to go step on the fucking guy and I realize—"

Ring ring ring.

"Shit. Hold my place."

The call lasted less than a minute.

"I gotta split. Can I borrow you for a few minutes?"

I never found out what was realized on the Bowery or who the old man was. Lou was on to something else. I agreed to let him borrow me for a few minutes. What I would eventually realize was that he was very afraid of being alone and needed someone by his side at all times. I had suddenly become one of those trusted few.

fifteen

I had never been in a bar before. I should say I had never been in a bar without my father. He would bet baseball games with JR, a local bookie my dad went to grade school with. JR's office was in the Piper's Kilt, a little Irish pub in Woodside that I think is still open to this day.

The place Lou took me to was a narrow, dark joint near the 59th Street subway. It smelled like old beer, mold, cigarettes, and sweat. The bar was on the left side of the room as you entered. It was long and high. About a dozen men and no women sat on tall stools in quiet contemplation of alcohol, nicotine, and regret. Lit by strands of half-burned-out holiday lights along the length of the back of the bar: the ghosts of Christmas past.

There was a row of four or five red vinyl booths along the right side. They were all empty. The booth closest to the entrance was sealed off with tape. There was a hole the size of a toilet seat in one of its benches. The hole was stuffed with newspaper, matchbooks, empty cigarette packs, and broken glass. It looked like they were in no rush to repair it.

We sat in the rear booth, the pay phone and the bathrooms just beyond us. A jukebox stood right next to the phone. Lou sat on the bench facing the entrance, I sat opposite. He took out a pack of Marlboros and lit one up.

"You got any change? I want to play some music." He started combing through his thousand pockets.

"I have a quarter." I handed it to him.

"Get me a gin and tonic. And get yourself something too."

He stood up and took a deep drag. I waited for him to give me the currency to pay for his drink but that custom didn't seem to apply to his world.

"I don't have any more money on me," I said. I felt guilty that I couldn't buy the man a drink. Which made no sense, of course, since he asked me to accompany him as a favor, not to mention I was strictly prohibited by law from purchasing alcoholic beverages. I guess it was just the way he said it, like we were pals and had gone drinking together many times before. I felt very mature when I walked into the bar with him and now I was just a kid again. A measly, shrimpy kid who couldn't afford to buy his buddy a cocktail.

Lou stared at me like he had forgotten who I was and why I was there. "Oh." He said it like he regretted bringing me along. Then he took off his boot and searched inside. Finding nothing, he took off the other boot and extracted a crumpled bill. "Here ya go, and get some more quarters."

It was a ten-spot. I unfolded it and walked to the bar as Lou scanned the titles on the juke. The bartender came and stood across the bar from me.

"What can I get you?" He said it neither friendly nor unfriendly.

I hadn't done much drinking in my life and was not partial to any particular alcoholic beverage. I was sure the bartender would refuse me because of my age anyway, so I just ordered two gin and tonics. "And some quarters, please."

"How many?" His voice was scraped with years and years of booze and smoke.

"Two."

"Two quarters?"

"No, two gin and tonics."

"Yeah, I know, but how many quarters?"

"Umm . . . four, please."

Some fifties doo-wop started playing on the jukebox. It was sad. Sad and perfect for this afternoon. I've heard the tune many times since: "Angel Baby" by Rosie and the Originals. Every time it plays I go right back to the rear booth of the Subway Inn on that long gray day, with Lou's black-leather-covered back to me as he studies the songs on tap.

I brought the drinks and the change back to the booth. Lou was on the phone and it looked like he was faking a conversation. He was laughing, chatting, and smiling, but in this forced and stilted way. It seemed so phony to me that if I didn't know him, I would have taken him for a lunatic. A bona fide Creedmoor case who wandered the streets in deep discussions with invisible friends and enemies.

He hung up the phone and sat across from me. He was still smiling and drank half his gin and tonic in one big gulp.

"She'll be here in ten minutes," he told me, as if I had been in on the arrangements. I assumed it wasn't Rachel because he'd said she wouldn't be back till the next day. He gave me two quarters from his pile of change. "Play us some tunes. This is the best jukebox in the city. It's the only reason I come to this shithole. I mean, for a shithole it's a cozy shithole and I do happen to like shitholes."

He didn't say my name at all. I don't think he knew what it was anymore. Since that first night he hadn't called me anything but *kid* once in a while. I couldn't even remember if I'd told him my name or not, but it didn't matter to him anyway. He just needed somebody next to him.

I stood at the jukebox rolling through the many

songs and intimidated by the possibility that I would choose something Lou didn't like. I was not musically hip or savvy. My favorites were the Beatles and I listened to a lot of Top 40 stuff on the radio. I liked the Pink Floyd album *Wish You Were Here* but I only had it because I'd won a contest at King Karol's record store. They had a fishbowl of jelly beans and I made the closest guess of how many were inside. (I said 41,111 and the real amount was 42,505.) It was the only contest I'd ever won. So Pink Floyd was as cutting edge as I'd gotten. I had not been exposed to the underground scene and I really had no desire to seek it out.

I was at a loss and didn't know what to choose. I finally settled on "Mrs. Robinson," which I'd always liked a lot. I meant to punch B491 into the keypad but because I was so nervous and scared of fucking up, I mistakenly entered B419. I didn't even realize I had done it until I sat back down and Tiny Tim's "Tiptoe Through the Tulips" began to play.

Lou looked at me like I was something stuck to the bottom of his boot, like a wad of dog shit he was about to scrape off with a sharp stick. "Tiny Tim?? Did you play Tiny Tim??!!"

"No. It wasn't me. I played Simon and Garfun—"

"Tiny fucking Tim!!" He laughed his ass off, and with more good nature than I had ever seen from him.

Now he knew what my name was. I was no longer Matty, Jack, or Kid. I was now Tiny Tim and usually just plain Tim. That was what he called me from that day forward and he would never forget it. Soon the memory of how he came up with the name would fade and both he and Rachel assumed it was my real name.

I abhorred being called it but was too timid to protest or correct him. So Tim I became.

sixteen

I knew she was lying to me. It was a posture, a way to distance herself and rise above the things she did. She wasn't gathering experience for writing, no . . . Sorry, that's not completely true. She had a poetic soul. She was a writer, an artist in her heart, and eventually the horrible reality of what she was doing would become the raw material for whatever literary or artistic form or discipline she would dedicate herself to. I was convinced of that.

This may be putting the cart before the horse, though. She turned tricks because she was poor and it was a way to make money. But not every person who needs money is going to sell their ass or pussy.

No. Something has to bend you that way first. Add to that an example, an introduction, or a possibility, and you have all the necessary components. Motive, means, and opportunity.

My theory is that there was a damaged sexual component in her psyche somewhere; an uncle, her father, a family friend . . . somebody fucked her up. And most likely when she was very young. I'm sure she was always pretty, precocious, and smart; her consciousness lit up as far back as five or six years old. An easy and enticing prey for the disturbed and deplorable individuals who would exploit an innocent and defenseless little girl. There is no limit to the evils of the world and if you can imagine it, it's been done. And worse.

What I came to learn was that her sister Sonia (or Sanoo as she was called by her family) was her entry point into prostituting herself. Veronica's sister introduced her to three or four men (it wasn't any more than that) Sanoo had already tricked with. Veronica said they were men who worked at the newspaper with her sister. This was the big factory press where they printed the newspaper, not the offices where they wrote it.

Sanoo was a beauty like her sister, but where Veronica was slim and petite, Sanoo was curvy and voluptuous. She had worked at the newspaper for a few years and guys were always asking her out on dates. A lot of these men were married. Sanoo started sleeping with a few of her suitors and if they were generous enough she made it a semiregular thing. One or two of these guys would give her number to a friend and eventually she became popular enough to quit the newspaper, making the same amount of money working a fraction of the hours.

When the law of diminishing returns asserted its inevitable influence, Sanoo's dates would ask if *she* had any friends she could introduce them to. She couldn't come up with any girlfriends she thought would be interested in such an arrangement, but when she mentioned she had a sixteen-year-old sister who was as pretty as she was, well . . . it was music to their perverted ears.

Barry was a friend of one of the newspaper guys and a chef in a fancy steakhouse down near the fish market on the East River. (Veronica would later reveal that in truth Barry was a short-order cook in a shitty coffee shop near the ferry.) Barry lived with his mother on Morton Street in the Village in a fifth-floor walkup that had no doorbell or buzzer out front. You had to call him on the phone and then he'd throw keys out the window in a little white glove that "could have been peeled off of Mickey Mouse's arm." He had lived in the little apartment with his mother his entire life.

Mama Ro, as she was called in the neighborhood, would often travel to Schenectady to visit her sister over long holiday weekends like Memorial Day or Labor Day. Barry would take advantage of this temporary freedom by having a girl climb the five flights of stairs and pay him a visit.

Veronica said that Barry had a strange relationship with his dog, an old, unkempt bitch named Duchess. While Veronica would be getting dressed after doing whatever it was she did with Barry, she would watch as Duchess curled up next to her naked master. She said that Barry would stroke Duchess around her breasts (do dogs have breasts, or are they just considered nipples?) and between her hind legs.

"Just like the way he was stroking my body a few minutes before," Veronica added.

She went on to describe how Duchess began to tremble and breathe heavy and rapid, her tail wagging stiff and wild. And all the while Barry's glazed eyes would be fixed on Veronica as she zipped her jeans and put on her shoes. She said it looked like Duchess would be Barry's next lay as soon as she got paid and walked out the door.

I told her I was surprised that despite the debauched scenario she described, she returned to do more business with the twisted freak.

"When I write my book it'll all be worth it. I may even say that Barry would bring the dog into our sexual encounter in some debauched Roman-emperor kind of way."

I told her I didn't think there was any possibility of the Barry/Duchess romance being anything but debauched, and that it needed no embellishment at all if she wanted to include this tale of animal love in her collected stories of woe and misfortune.

"Don't diminish my truth." It was something she said often, like a mantra or an adopted maxim that you'd write on a piece of paper and tape to the mirror. "Okay? Don't diminish my truth."

"I'm not diminishing it at all. In fact, I'm encouraging you to stick to your truth, that your truth needs no dressing up or down, no manipulation necessary." I said it with a slightly sarcastic inflection, a tone I regret to this day.

"I told you when we first got to know each other that I'm a nigger of the world, I live outside of society, and I have no tolerance for anyone who judges me. Did you forget I said that?"

"I'm not judging you at all." I was lying. "I am judging Harry or Barry or Larry or whatever the dog-fucker's name is."

She stared at me cold and hard. "I can't say for sure what he did to the dog, how far he went, and that's not the point here. I never had a dog so I don't have a context as to what is or isn't normal and what lines if any were crossed. Maybe it was just me being uncomfortable and twisting what he did into something wrong and immoral." She was defending the bastard. She wanted to make claim to the depravity as a trial she'd endured but at the same time she was downplaying the perversity to win the argument against me.

"It's not you, it's him, and it's not normal, it's abuse, sexual abuse, and it takes a certain type of sick, psychopathic mind to commit sexual abuse. I had a dog, a female dog named Christmas, and the thought of fondling her never entered my mind, ever."

"Maybe you should have. Maybe it would have made you a more interesting human being." The corners of her mouth were pinched downward in a way I'd never seen. It was like a Venetian carnival mask she took out solely for special festivals of indignation.

We finally reached the entrance to the 59th Street subway station. She turned to me slowly and stared into my eyes. I thought it was a strange moment for her to want to kiss me.

"You bore me."

I was right, a kiss was far from her intention.

"You bore me." Three words said flatly before she walked down the stairs and left me standing there feeling like a jilted husband. She had chosen a bestiality-bent ingrate over me. I had those odd soda-bubble butterflies in my gut, the kind I'd get as a little boy right before I'd start to cry. I did not want to be seventeen years old and crying on 60th Street in the middle of the afternoon. So I started spitting.

I spat on the sidewalk like it was sick dogfucking Barry's face and maybe even *her* face if she ever treated me this way again. No. I would never have the courage to do that to her. Never.

I spit until the butterflies went away and I felt certain the tears were not going to come. I spit the whole way home.

seventeen

Whoever it was Lou was waiting for finally arrived. She was a short, wiry young woman with close-cropped but unevenly cut blond hair. Very similar in style to Lou's. She wore a baggy black suit which gave the impression of a little kid playing dress-up with her father's clothing. She smelled like booze, Old Spice, Doublemint gum (which she chewed non-stop), and cigarettes.

Lou didn't introduce us. I watched them greet each other and sipped my gin and tonic. The taste reminded me of something I couldn't put my finger on.

"Mona, Mona, Mona, Mona!" He kissed her on both cheeks with his lips pursed into a ridiculous tiny circle, then allowed her to slide into the booth next to him. He made it a point to always be in the outside seat.

She settled onto the vinyl bench and started talking like she had just come back from a bathroom break and was resuming a conversation that had been going on for hours: "I'm not calling her back. She wants to be First Lady and put on airs, that's fine for whoever, but don't think I'm gonna kiss fucking ass. She forgets who brought her around in the first place."

Lou didn't seem to be paying much attention to what she was saying. "Do you want a drink, Mona? Hey, Tim, get us another round."

This time he held up a handful of bills. He gave me a ten and shoved the rest into Mona's right hand, which simultaneously passed a small fold of tinfoil into his left hand. Springing to life, he dashed to the bathroom and disappeared. Mona took Lou's pack of Marlboros and all the coins he'd left on the table. She stuck them in the big pockets of her suit jacket and sealed herself into the phone booth. I finished my drink and went to the bar to order another round. I felt high and happy and wanted a cigarette even though I wasn't a smoker. The alcohol buzzed me enough courage to ask a leathery-skinned man with a fallen face for a cigarette. He looked at me sideways as he sipped something brown from a small glass. Then he slid his pack of Benson & Hedges toward me.

"Here ya go, champ." Champ was much better than Tim. He seemed happy to offer me the smoke and insisted on lighting it for me. I sucked it hard as the flame ignited the paper and tobacco. A big draft of smoke filled my throat and lungs. I was suffocating as I tried to hold it in, and then I let it all out in a fit of coughs, hacks, and gags.

"Easy does it, buckaroo." From deep in his throat came a long, wheezy, and phlegmy laugh. I kept on coughing and retching and must have turned green. The more I choked, the more he laughed. The bartender joined in the hilarity as he chuckled his way over to me with three gin and tonics. When I regained my composure, I handed the cigarette back to its original owner, who raised both hands over his head like I was mugging him at gunpoint.

"I don't want it. Why don't you save it for a rainy day." Another thick mucous laugh followed. "Maybe when you get a little hair on your balls."

I had gone from champ to buckaroo to prepubescent. I killed the cigarette, smothering the life out of it, and grabbed the drinks.

When I returned to the booth, Mona and Lou were nowhere to be found. The phone booth was empty and I was alone. "Duke of Earl" began playing on the jukebox: *"Duke, Duke, Duke, Duke of Earl, Earl, Earl, Duke of Earl, Earl, Earl, Duke of Earl . . ."* It was not my selection but I wished I could take the credit. For it was brilliant: yes, the song of course, but the choice of it in that very instant equally genius and in perfect harmony with the time, the place, the mood, the lights, the musty stench of the bar in its melancholic, intoxicated East Side afternoon. It was Lou's choice. Had to be.

I figured they were both in the bathroom, which distressed me because I felt like maybe I was going to puke. The smoke, tar, and nicotine weren't sitting right with the gin. I was a rank amateur when it came to drugs, booze, sex, cigarettes, and rock and roll. This was not to remain the case for much longer, I thought, as I started on the second gin and tonic of my life. I took a big slug. It went down smooth and easy and seemed to have a positive effect on the nausea. "Duke of Earl" began to take me back to my father's black Cadillac speeding along the Westside Highway near the George Washington Bridge, on our way home from his uncle Otto's house in Fort Lee, New Jersey. Me riding shotgun with no seat belt, the car reeking of Optimo Cigarillos and the lights of the city having just come up as the summer sun went down.

I wasn't going to puke after all. I started to feel good and buzzed. Excited at the evening and the city, both open and unwritten before me. I was hoping Lou would emerge from the bathroom and take me to his next destination: another dive bar or some strange apartment where we'd continue our adventures together.

Mona came out of the bathroom, walking right

past me and the drink I had waiting for her. Her head and limbs were moving like she was in a heated conversation with someone, but no words or sounds came out of her mouth. I watched her back as she walked out the front door and onto East 61st Street. "Duke of Earl" ended. I drained drink number two.

I think Frank Sinatra came on the juke next but I'm not positive. It could have been someone else. I don't know much about Sinatra and his music. I started to drink Mona's cocktail. Halfway into the song and still no sign of Lou. He had been gone long enough that it started to worry me, but I was afraid to go into the bathroom to look for him. I was pretty sure his long absence had something to do with the folded tinfoil that Mona gave him but I had no idea what that really meant or what I would find him doing in there.

I waited for Sinatra or whoever to finish and then the Allman Brothers started playing. A short, stout, redheaded guy with a beard started grooving to the music as he perched on his barstool. It was a long song and I finished Mona's drink as the extended and boring instrumental break went on and on. That made three gin and tonics gone down my hatch. My body started to feel heavy. I became hyperaware of how I moved my arms and how the weight of my body would redistribute itself every time I shifted in my seat.

When the Allman song was finished there was a long silence in the bar. It was a menacing and unsettling quiet. No music, no talking, only the clinking of bottles as the bartender restocked beer. Creepy. Like the lights had come up at closing time and revealed the depths of all our misery and loneliness. I was hit with a big wave of sadness which lingered for a few minutes until I was hit with an even bigger wave of terror. I was convinced Lou would never come out of the bathroom. That he was dead; an overdose, and I was somehow responsible. I was an accessory to suicide which meant murder since another person was involved: me. I would never return home and would spend the next few decades in prison.

Elton John broke the silence with his "Goodbye Yellow Brick Road." This was unbearable. The Yellow Brick Road was my life as I had known it up until now, but it was time to say goodbye. Things would never be the same again. My life was over and maybe it would be better if I made sure of it by jumping off the 59th Street Bridge. Death was preferable to life in prison, and the bridge was only a few blocks away.

eighteen

Two weeks after the Barry Dogfucker incident, Veronica officially summoned me out of exile. There was a seldom-used back door near the southwest corner of our school. It opened onto a filthy alley where rats scurried and people pissed. I used it daily as a means of avoiding as many of my fellow students as possible.

Veronica was waiting for me in the alley wearing white-framed sunglasses. She was standing there with her arms folded, smirking like she knew the exact second I would be walking through the door.

"Do you have any desire to redeem yourself?"

It was the first sentence she had spoken to me in fifteen days. I didn't miss a beat and immediately said yes. It would be one of the great mistakes of my life and something I'm sure I will regret till the grave.

We took the subway downtown to Astor Place and wound our way through the East Village streets. We finally came to a stop at a small storefront on East 4th, 5th, or 6th Street. Somewhere near First Avenue or Avenue A.

"This is just to prove to you that what I said before is true and to remove any doubts you may have about me. I want all of that cleared out of the way before we go any further."

We entered the little store. It was a narrow strip of a shop that sold occult books and objects used for rituals, rites, and spells. A store that catered to practitioners of witchcraft, Wicca, Satan worship, black magic, white magic, voodoo, Santeria, and I think maybe even Buddhism or Hinduism.

The aromas of burned hair, pine trees, clove, roses, and tobacco hung in the air. Air that had grown thick from years of desperate aspirations: some fulfilled, some fruitless, most of them malicious. It took more than the usual effort to move my body in its normal fashion; I experienced an underwater, heavy gravity feeling and grew light-headed. I was also afraid, fearful of falling under the negative and dark influences that through osmosis had permeated everything I laid eyes upon, including the stained wall, dirty floor, and cobwebbed ceiling.

There was a large glass case that displayed a variety of ritual robes, garments, hoods, and hats. Their colors, shapes, and insignias blasphemous and sacrilegious, in deliberate perversions of Christian and Jewish traditions. On a shelf were a selection of idols made in the different images of Satan, above which were a row of crosses nailed into place upside down.

On the walls there were painted astrological and occult symbols, mostly in black or red, and framed pictures, drawings, and charts of names, glyphs, spell recipes, and images of unknown dark saints.

There were lots and lots of candles of every size, color, and shape, the majority black and phallic, rendered in obscene dimension and detail.

Veronica casually told me that her aunt Myra was the owner of the shop. Myra inherited it from her master who had passed on five years ago. The one person working behind the counter was a small woman with mousy brown hair and tortoiseshell glasses. She presented no outer appearance of witch or satanist and showed no recognition of Veronica. She ignored us and was engrossed in the latest issue of *Rolling Stone* magazine, which featured Donny Osmond on its cover.

Veronica pulled a slim book off a shelf. She held it between her hands for a few seconds and closed her eyes. Then she handed it to me. The soft slick covers both front and rear were all black except for four or five Latin-seeming words. She put her hands over mine and pressed them all together with the book in the center of the sandwich.

"Can you feel its power?"

I tried to but I didn't. I didn't feel anything at all

emanating from the book. Besides the heavy atmospheric pressure in the store, the only power I felt came from her and her alone—a magnetic polar pull and centrifugal force that I was helpless against. I held the book tightly, closed my eyes, and pretended to feel whatever it was she wanted me to feel. She laughed, took it from my hands, and put it back on the shelf.

"I want to buy you a gift. Is that okay?" she asked.

Anything was okay. Whatever she did, whatever she would ask of me, wherever she wanted to go, I was at her mercy. And though I was scared shitless in the narrow confines of the hellish little shop, it was still heaven to be by her side.

I wanted to hold her hand but was afraid of fucking things up. She hadn't looked in my direction for over two weeks and I didn't want to upset the delicate balance required to remain in her favor. I followed her to a long glass case that displayed an array of rings, pendants, amulets, crystals, bracelets, wands, and scepters. Some of the items looked like they were very expensive, made of gold or silver, and adorned with precious-looking stones and jewels.

"I want you to wait for me outside."

"Okay." I left without asking why. I tried to peek through the window but the heavy black curtains didn't leave any crack for me to see what she was doing.

She emerged smiling after a few minutes and extended a little black box toward me. "For you."

Inside the box was a small silver runic symbol attached to a fine metal chain. It had the shape of a capital Y but the bottom line extended all the way up, bisecting the v at the top and forming an upward-pointing trident.

She called it an *Algiz* and said it was a shield of protection that warded off evil. It also gave its wearer the ability to "channel one's energies appropriately," but she did not elaborate on what that meant or how I would go about doing so.

I wanted to ask her what she thought I needed protection from or what specific evil was being warded off, but all I could muster was "Thank you" as she fastened the clasp behind my neck. She then showed me the exact same symbol hanging from her own neck. I had never noticed it on her before.

"A very special person gave me mine. By giving you yours, I extend the chain of connection."

"A very special person gave me mine too." I meant it sincerely.

Her thoughtfulness and care opened something in me. As we walked toward Second Avenue my thoughts began to speed up. But instead of anxiety and confusion, my mind was infused with sharpness and clarity. Thoughts were coming fast but I was able to see them and digest them one by one as they passed through my mind. It was like I was decoding the mysterious logic that made one thought lead to and give way to the next, the mechanism behind my mind revealing itself for the first time in my life.

Everything made sense—the shape of her eyes and the lines of mascara around it were perfect cosmic geometry. The molecules that made up her scarf vibrated at the right speed and frequency to create the only color that could possibly express who she was at this very moment. The deep violet fabric twisted around her long neck, not slack and not tight—just how it should be. Exactly where it belonged. Just like me.

nineteen

I stood up and it felt like I was on a boat. I took a deep breath. My legs felt like they were sinking into thick, sucking mud. I had to take each step with care and precision to avoid falling flat on my face. Walking to the bathroom must have taken me fifteen minutes at the pace I was going. It didn't really matter at that point; once I confirmed my friend's death, I was heading to the bridge.

The door to the bathroom was unlocked so I pushed it open. There was a small sink beneath a broken mirror to my left and a low urinal just beyond. At the rear was a single toilet stall, its heavy black door closed. I could see Lou's boots in the gap between the bottom of the door and the floor. The way the boots were situated made me think he was standing up and facing the rear wall; I took that as a good sign.

I knocked gently and spoke softly: "Hey, Lou, are you okay?"

"Who's askin'?"

"It's me. Tim." I could have easily said my real

name but I was afraid of confusing him. It didn't bother me—him still being alive meant I didn't have to jump off the bridge. Under the circumstances he could have called me Shirley and I would have been fine with it.

"What can I do for you, Tim?"

"Nothing, I'm just checking on you. You've been in here a long time."

"Have I?"

"Kind of. Your friend left."

"To which friend do you refer?"

"Mona. She's gone."

"That nasty cunt's no friend of mine. She's a treacherous leper. Stay clear of trash like that."

"I will." There was silence between us for a few beats. I was holding onto the wall to my right to keep myself vertical. It was a struggle. "Are you okay, Lou?" I really wanted to get the hell home but I wouldn't be able to make it without his help.

"I am outstanding, Tim. Just fantastic. Come on in."

He opened the door and looked at me with a big stretched-out smile that pulled his eyes toward the sides of his head. The pair seemed to be moving independently of each other as they scanned the corners of the room behind me and then every inch of my person up and down. And all in a fraction of a second. He held a black marker in his hand.

"If I was a scientist, and in many ways I am just that, I would publish it and win the Nobel fucking Prize."

The wall was covered in black-inked script from about waist level to up above his head. At the very top were the biggest words: *DOUBT = FEAR = CANCER = DEATH*. It appeared to be the title of a monograph that he had composed on this toilet stall wall. The print of the remaining lines was smaller.

Contrary to popular belief, I am no angel of mercy nor am I a mercenary who has battled and slain for the worthless illusions of public recognition and approval. When the tides of popular opinion inevitably turned against me, my detractors began a systematic campaign to debunk, destroy, and persecute. And all this in the name of artistic criterion and aesthetic quantification. I laugh every day at their efforts in futility and the sterile seeds of self-loathing they attempted to plant into the fertile earth that is my mind. Self-hatred turned outward toward an object (me). A projection of their own personal internalized disgust for the limitations of their own minuscule intellect, stunted emotional expression, and defective humanity. I am convinced that the DOUBT of which I speak is the very agent of DEATH and destruction that we call CANCER. They are one and the same. When the jewel that is one's own unique individuality is stifled, its growth stunted, and its nature ignored, the cellular structure that underlies the entire biological, psychic, and spiritual system has no choice but to turn on itself in fierce rebellion and retaliation, precipitating an unstoppable chain of metastatically catastrophizing events. These calamities are of course not limited to the singular isolated human being. They can of course become pandemic in a home, a state, a nation, and as future generations will undoubtedly witness . . . on a global planetary scale . . . perhaps even beyond the boundaries of our beloved earth. Nothing in the universe is immune.

"I'm done. I just have to sign it," he said as he took the cap off the marker and crouched down. He scribbled his name and jerked upright with shocking speed. Handing the marker over to me, he said: "You sign it too, Tim. After all, you inspired it." He left me alone in the stall and went back into the bar.

I had no idea what I'd said or done to inspire his theory but I scrawled *Tiny Tim* in neat print right below his name. Then I copied the whole thing onto some wads of paper towels. I still have them. They live pressed between the pages of the huge *Webster's Dictionary* my father bought me when I started the eighth grade.

I did not copy the schematic drawing of a con-
centration camp that Lou had made on the adjacent
wall. This he had titled *Eichmannn* (sic) *Industrial, Inc.*
Below the illustration was a "qualitative comparison" of Zyklon B and napalm. This segued into a
conspiratorial link between Dow Chemicals and the
Third Reich, the details of which are now lost to the
ages.

twenty

We strolled the streets in silence. Everything around us—all the sights, sounds, smells, tastes—had a specific place in the new consciousness that had possessed me. The noxious exhaust from the cabs and buses; the dog shit in a pile near the curb; the ancient, hunchbacked woman who moved slow and steady with eyes straight down like she was crossing a stream that flowed through the middle of Avenue A; the siren of the ambulance delivering a bleeding boy who'd fallen down a flight of stone stairs; the laughter of a toothless beggar whose eyes revealed despair—all of it made sense somehow. It was all one singular thing: the good, the bad, the revolting, the repulsive, the joyous, the beautiful, the fortunate, the suffering, and then Veronica and myself. All filling the same frame and telling one singular story. A story that was forever in the middle, without beginning or end; an eternal folding and unfolding of events.

We sat in a café and ate falafels in pita. Through the lens of my expanded mind it was the most logical, delicious, and perfect food one could consume. Each component synchronized and synthesized into a complete, unified, and seamless thingness. The smoothness of the tahini with the crunch of the fried falafel, the softness of the airy pita bread with the crispness of the lettuce and carrots, the burn of the hot sauce with the sharpness of the onions: each part an absolute necessity to complete the harmonics. The sandwich was a microcosm of me and Veronica together in the macrocosm of New York City and all the universe beyond.

Veronica wiped some tahini off the corner of her mouth, then touched her Algiz and looked at me. "So now that we're united in protection, are you willing to step out into the dark unknown with me?"

In an instant I crashed back into real-time regular thought: the old and familiar reality. My nonordinary perception was done and gone as if it never existed at all. In hindsight, I'm surprised her question failed to send chills or sound an alarm or siren in warning of the events to come. The way it came out of her mouth, it sounded solemn and earnest, a call to arms.

"It's the opportunity for redemption that I mentioned. I still have the highest of hopes for you."

"I'm in," I replied.

In my heart I wasn't so sure why I had to redeem

myself or what I had done that made any redemption necessary. I assumed it had something to do with my reaction to her telling me about tricking with Barry. I should have explained that what I said to her wasn't meant to be an assault or judgment on her character or the things she chose to do, and that my feelings came from a place of solidarity, respect, and care. I was being protective; she was still technically a minor, a child in the eyes of the law. It was her john who was committing a repulsive act both illegal and immoral.

But I didn't say any of this. I said nothing at all. She was right and I was wrong. She was superintelligent, sophisticated, streetwise, mature, and mystical. I was none of the above, so I moved to whatever music she chose on her jukebox.

And that was fine by me. I would have followed her down into the sewer and stayed at her side until she was ready to come up for air.

twenty-one

Shortly after I was formally dubbed Tim, Lou gave me an unsealed envelope with a folded piece of paper inside. The envelope was addressed to a man in care of a music magazine located in Los Angeles. He told me to keep the letter until he was ready to send it and that I was welcome to read it but might be better off if I didn't.

"Be sure to wash your hands after, if you do read it." He laughed. "Better yet, wear gloves."

He explained that he was afraid of the force contained within the envelope and that once unleashed on its target, some of its destructive powers could leak out into the world. This energy had the capability to alter the angle of the earth's axis, so he wasn't sure if he was ever going to send it. I was to keep it in a safe place and await further instructions from him.

I, of course, read the letter despite the warnings. It was handwritten in a manic, rabid print, each word tightly compacted and compressed though the spaces between were generous. He had done things to the page itself. I'd rather not say what I imagine he did (it involved bodily fluids) but nevertheless I'm glad I listened to him and wore the suggested gloves, which in my case were mittens.

Before reading the letter, however, I asked Lou what had prompted him to write it. He said the intended recipient had published some extremely cruel and inhumane things about Rachel in a magazine article about Lou's last record.

The following was Lou's defense of his lady's honor:

January 15, 1977
446 East 52nd Street
New York, NY 10022

Dear Unesteemed Journalistic Scum Slash Shallow Size Queen:

I hereby supplicate: through truest intent, purest pledge, duly sworn oath, and most high prayer; all the gods and demons who lit the fires, dropped the frogs, and pissed the blood, who sent the swarms of locusts, malarial fleas, and poxéd lice upon the house of Rameses.

I beseech them to dump the turds of a million infectious buzzards upon your head; the feces infused with the syphilitic pus and madness of all the dead whores of Babylon and Baghdad.

May the facsimile of manhood that lies between your legs wither, fester, and decay like the corpses that filled the pits of Buchenwald and Birkenau.

May your manqué genitalia become a faucet and font of the most fetid and diseased sewage ever to seep quiet through the veins of Calcutta and black-plagued London.

And all the evils of the Aztec Heart Eaters, the thousand and one Arabian Sahars, the most abhorrent, obscene, defiling, and profane spells and incantations in the entire canon of Haddo's left-handed path, the Yamas, Yantras, Maras, and Mataris, the second face of Mordrake, the 107 adventitious stains, the 909 untimely Turkish deaths, the 51 omens of Jephthah, the hex of the 66 hairs: may they ceaselessly bear their malevolent and wicked fruit upon you and your house for generation upon generation uninterrupted.

GET THE PICTURE, MOTHERFUCKER?

From this day forth I strictly and explicitly forbid you to hear any sound I have ever uttered, created, or recorded, either spoken word or musical note, whether voice my own or instrument born.

For you and yours I now render and infuse every note, riff, vibration, every syllable, with the potentiality described above.

YOU ARE FOREWARNED.

BEWARE.

DON'T SAY I DIDN'T TELL YOU.

YOU WILL REAP TEARS FROM THE FILTH YOU HAVE SOWN.

And happier I could not be.

Yours in Hate,
(here he scrawled his indecipherable signature)

Lou never mentioned the letter after he gave it to me that day. It remains in my possession but is now sealed.

twenty-two

We stood on the corner of Second Avenue and 1st Street. Veronica said we were waiting for one of her sister's friends. I had a good idea what she meant by this but was not sure how I was going to fit into the picture. I asked her if it was Barry. She shook her head and stared me down.

"You're not gonna chicken out on me, are you? I can trust you to handle yourself and watch my back, right?"

"Of course you can." Even though I had no idea what I was agreeing to and ignorant of what support I was offering.

"If you want to back out, please do it now. I'll understand and won't think any less of you. I promise."

But I knew if I were to retreat she would never speak to me again, my cowardice a permanent black mark. Banished for life.

"I'm with you. I'll go wherever you need to. Just tell me where it is we're going."

"Uptown. To someone's house. He's picking us up any minute. I don't want to go into details, but if you're willing, I don't think you'll regret it."

"I'm willing. I would just rather have some idea of what it is you need me to do." This was as forceful and assertive as I'd been all day.

She leaned in and kissed me, grabbing both my arms below the shoulders and pulling me in close. She kept her lips against mine for a long time and though she pressed them tightly, they were soft and relaxed.

And everything about it was right: the grip of her hands as they dug into my arms, the temperature of her mouth, the taste of its moisture, the smell of her face and hair, the pounds per square inch of pressure between her lips and mine, the tension in her tongue. Everything as it should be.

When she finally pulled away, she did it slowly and gradually. With our heads a safe distance apart, she looked into my eyes and said: "You're my work in progress. And coming along quite nicely."

A small white car pulled up to the corner where we stood. Veronica looked to the driver and gave a little wave. Even though it was starting to get dark, I could see the features of the lone person inside the car, behind the wheel. He was in his thirties and had long, dark, shaggy curls on the sides and back of his head. The hair on top was cut shorter. He had a thin mustache and a small triangle of a beard below his bottom lip. He smiled at Veronica with a tight little grin. I disliked him immediately.

Veronica grabbed my hand and led me to the two-door Honda. The driver reached over and unlocked the passenger side. Veronica swung it open and the man reached back, pulled a lever, and pushed the front seat forward. Veronica and I climbed into the back. The man returned the seat to its proper place, sealing us in the back without access to the door handle. He stepped on the gas and pulled away from the curb.

"Hi, Smitty, this is Matt," she said as she squeezed my knee, reassuring me that all would be okay.

"Hi, Matt. I'm Smitty . . . Do you like beer?" He had a thin, reedy, asthmatic voice.

I turned to look at Veronica.

"I don't," she said.

"Me neither," I added.

"Okay. We'll go straight home then. I got soda and chips." He stared at me through the rearview mirror. His eyes were small and narrowly spaced behind wire-rimmed granny glasses.

"I like gin," I said. The confidence in my voice surprised me. I think it surprised Veronica too. She squeezed my knee even tighter.

Smitty looked at me again. He was sizing me up, I could feel it. "With tonic and lime?" he asked.

"Just tonic is fine." I grabbed Veronica's hand as we turned onto Houston Street on our way west.

twenty-three

Lou would never forget the name he created for me. But he would always forget that I lived in the same building he did.

"Tim, what are you doing here?"

I was waiting for the elevator in the lobby. He came up from the storage bins in the basement holding some small cardboard boxes. I was about to explain to him, for the fourth or fifth time, that I lived on the sixth floor, but before I could he put his hand on my shoulder.

"Can you come up and see me later on? I need help with an amplifier." Lou was out the front door before I could reply.

A few hours later I stood at the threshold to his apartment on the eighth floor. The door was halfway open but I could see them both in the living room. I knocked on the jamb but neither one heard me. They were in the exact same positions as the first time I was there. Except this time Rachel's head was tilted down and her shoulders were shaking a little bit.

Lou was at the reel-to-reel deck which sat on the

low table in the middle of the room. He was play-ing a fifteen-second stretch of tape over and over. It sounded like the strangulation and mutilation of a dozen guitars in a room with a hundred radios and TV sets all tuned to different frequencies of static. It was the sound of the city itself, distorted through a fish-eye lens and held to the eye of a man who'd been up for five days straight on some godforsaken strain of chemical stimulant. All violence, paranoia, and apocalyptic terror.

"Can you hear that, babe? Can you hear it con-structing itself? A melody perfect and self-arisen out of the ether. Like the iron filings between the plastic cover and the drawing of the farmer's face. You know the toy I mean? Woolly Billy . . . Willy Bully . . . You push the magnetic pencil around and pull the filings into the form of a beard or a mustache? . . . It's like that only it's automatic, happening on its own accord, out of complete randomness . . . Do you understand what that means? . . . What I've proven? . . . Melody existing as a primal force in the universe, inherent in nature, underlying and permeating the mitochon-dria of cells, lying dormant under existence itself . . . Can you hear it, babe? Can you hear the beauty? The innate intelligence of organized sound completely independent from the mind of man. Fucking Mozart would be jealous, and I'm not comparing me to him 'cause it's not me who did it . . . IT'S SIMPLY THERE . . . always was and will be . . . We have to be careful here . . . I have to be very cautious how I go about this . . . the FBI, the FCC, without a doubt they've banned some of these frequencies . . . they keep these beauties for themselves and the CIA . . . they must be on a list somewhere in Washington . . . subversive potentialities. Extraterrestrial intelligence, sound arranged by sound itself, by nature and electricity . . . positive and negative ions, the celestial poles!! . . . Do you know what this proves??!"

I had arrived at a critical point. Lou was Dr. Frankenstein, minutes after the slabbed cadaver was lowered from the sky where it bathed in the fires of heaven. Salivating at the smell of charred meat, he pressed his stethoscope to the Monster's chest and heard the *lub-dub* of its borrowed heart. Life! A corpse no more!

"There's clarity beneath all the chaos of the universe and this is the empirical evidence." As the words fell from his mouth, he saw me in the doorway.

"Tim me boy!" He stood up, kissed me on the head, and told me to have a seat. I sat cross-legged on the floor right across the table from where he was sitting. Rachel didn't move at all, I wasn't sure if she knew I was there. I could see that tears were flowing down her face, smudging her black mascara and streaking crooked lines down her Cherokee cheekbones.

"What are you doing here, Tim?"

"You told me you needed help with an amplifier."

"I did? . . . I do. Yes. I told you that today, right?"

"Yes, a few hours ago."

"Right, right. It's over here." He pointed to a corner of the room where a hulk of rectangular something was covered in a white sheet. He unveiled it, revealing a gargantuan speaker cabinet and amplifier head. It sat there big and menacing.

"Did you bring a dolly? We're gonna need a dolly."

Before I could tell him I didn't have a dolly, Rachel stood up and started shouting what I figured were Spanish curse words. She didn't look at either Lou or myself, she just marched away. As she continued her tirade, things started to get smashed inside the bedroom.

Lou chuckled and shook his head. "Can't live with 'em, can't live without 'em." He put a fatherly arm around my shoulder. "Do you have a girlfriend, Tim?"

"I do . . . kind of."

"Well, here's the secret to the fairer sex," he said, unfazed as another crash erupted. "What I'm going to tell you is the law of the jungle and there's no way around it, so it's best you learn it now. Okay?

. . . In essence it's very simple . . . here it is . . . *You can't win*. That's it. Get it? . . . When it comes to an argument, a disagreement? Forget it . . . *You can't win* . . . It's impossible. The other thing is, when a problem or an issue arises, a woman wants to be heard, she wants her feeling understood. But a man wants to fix it, he immediately wants to find a solution . . . but that's not important to the woman in the midst of her emotions and feelings. No! She simply wants to be listened to."

He paused as something made of glass hit the bedroom door and shattered. He smiled.

"She is so beautiful, man. She is a genius." His head was turned toward me but his eyes were scouring the room like they were following the path of a mosquito. "So, Tim my man, once you understand the rules, once you accept it as truth, life becomes a whole lot easier . . . Got a cigarette?"

"No. I don't. Sorry."

"That's okay, Tim. That is *okay* . . ." Lou patted the amplifier. "Now how the fuck we gonna get this thing into a cab?"

There was no way on earth we were getting it into a cab.

"I think we need a van or a truck, Lou."

"What about a station wagon? Would a station wagon work?" he said as he dashed to his bright red telephone. He picked up the receiver, dialed three numbers, and paused.

"A station wagon would probably be okay," I said without really being sure.

Loud hammering came from the bedroom. Lou shook his head, smiling again, and said as if to himself: "I tell you, man, she is something else. Just brilliant. Nothing short of a philosopher queen." He hung up the phone and continued, now directly to me: "Okay . . . where can we get a station wagon today? My van guy broke his driving foot jumping out a window. He's afraid to get behind the wheel till his cast comes off."

"I don't know. Ciro has a van, maybe you can ask him. He always says you're a good customer. Last week he loaned it to the Egyptian guy who owns the newsstand on the corner."

"That's great, Tim. Yes. Good idea. Who's Zero?"

"Ciro. My boss. The guy who owns the diner."

"Of course! Zero! I know Zero. That guy's probably seen more breakfasts than a gynecologist."

Lou laughed at his own joke. It seemed funny when it came out of his mouth but when I broke it down and tried to understand the logic of it, I was at a loss. Still am.

"Yeah, that would be perfect. Ask Zero if we can borrow it. You can use the Batphone. Would you like a drink?"

The bedroom was quiet as I dialed the diner. Lou started pouring gin into two tall glasses.

"No tonic, Tim. Sorry." He topped the gin off with Coca-Cola. A god-awful combination but Lou didn't seem to mind. He drained half his glass before Ciro answered the phone.

I had to think on my feet. I had lied to Lou when I told him that Ciro thought he was a good customer. I don't know why I said it, it just came out of my mouth. The truth was that Ciro considered Lou and Rachel "a pair of junkie freaks." His nickname for them was "Dr. Heckle and Mrs. Jekyl." Ciro wouldn't give them a dishrag if they weren't paying for it.

Fortunately, Lou got absorbed in ransacking his kitchen in search of an important phone number he had misplaced. So I told Ciro that my mother needed the van for an hour to pick up a new dining room table.

Ciro was happy to do my mother a favor. I think he had a little crush on her. He was overly kind and a little flirty whenever she was in the diner and always gave her a free black-and-white cookie for dessert. And I don't think it was out of respect for me.

I got off the phone victorious and told Lou we had a van. I would go to the diner, pick up the keys, and Lou could meet me and the van in the parking lot on Second Avenue.

"Fantastic." He swallowed the rest of his gin in a single swig. "Just pull it up in front of the building. I'll ask Rogelio if he has a dolly," he said as he poured himself a fresh one.

Wait. Did I hear him correctly? Pull it up in front of the building? How was I supposed to do that? I didn't have a driver's license nor had I ever driven a car on an actual road. The little driving experience I had outside of the bumper cars in Adventureland was with my dad in the huge, empty parking lot of Shea Stadium about two years ago. That's it. The idea of me navigating a van through the streets of rush-hour Manhattan was ridiculous.

I worked up a bit of courage and said: "Uhhhhm, maybe it's better if you do the driving, Lou. I don't have a license."

"Nonsense, Tim. I have complete faith in your ability to handle a vehicle. Besides, if you don't do it, we're stuck. I never, ever drive. Too many near-death calls. You're a smart kid, you'll do fine. And we're not going very far at all. Just a few blocks. Piece of cake." He said this while still looking for the number he so desperately needed. His limbs and torso seemed to be running on separate motors all working independently of each other. As their RPMs increased, he scratched, jerked, and twitched through the kitchen, his search becoming more hopeless by the second.

twenty-four

Smitty lived on the far Upper West Side of Manhattan. Washington Heights or Inwood, I think, maybe near Dyckman Street. He spent about half an hour trying to squeeze into a parking space that was impossible to accommodate his shitty little white car. This led to another half hour or so of cruising his neighborhood until he finally came upon a Puerto Rican family who were loading into a gray Ford. They must have been going to the airport because they put three huge suitcases and four smaller bags into the trunk. The grandma had to be helped by two younger women and the walk from the entrance to their building to the car took an eternity.

Neither Veronica nor myself spoke at all during the whole parking ordeal. Smitty took all the waiting in patient stride; it must have been a daily routine of sorts for him. All he said was, "Easy does it, abuelita," over and over until grandma was securely stowed in the backseat and her door was closed and locked.

Finally, the gray four-door Ford with passengers

bound for Ponce, PR, mercifully pulled out and onto Broadway, allowing Smitty to slide his slimy Civic into the void. I couldn't figure out how to push the seat up so we could free ourselves from the tiny rear of the Honda and was forced to suffer the indignity of waiting for Smitty to pull the latch and move the seat forward, his head almost touching mine but his eyes fixed on Veronica.

When we were standing on the sidewalk Smitty cleared his throat, wiped his forehead with a handkerchief, and said: "You guys want pretzels or peanuts? I got chips. Barbecue."

"I'm good," Veronica said as she ran her fingers through her hair. I didn't say a word. Smitty just nodded and started to walk up Broadway. We followed.

His apartment was on the third floor. The elevator was not working or was stuck on some other floor so we walked up the stone steps in a counter-clockwise-winding ascent, our footsteps loud and echoing in the stairwell. There was a strong, wet smell of mold during the climb but as we stepped through the door into the third-floor hallway, the stench was eclipsed by the noxious combo of boiling animal innards and piss. This foul scent seemed to lessen as we approached Smitty's door at the far end of the hallway. He put the key in the hole and invited us into apartment 3NW.

There was nothing at all masculine about Smitty's one-room flat. If he had told me that it was an old lady's apartment, I would have believed it. It was very spare, neat, and orderly, but dusty and stuffy as well. The windows, which were filthy, looked like they hadn't been opened in decades. The rugs and furniture were old and worn and there was nothing personal anywhere. No books, no photos, no diploma. No posters, paintings, or religious objects. It was slightly more homey than a hotel room, mostly thanks to a colorful knit-wool blanket folded in half on top of the bed.

"Make yourselves at home."

Smitty went into the alcove that was his kitchen. There was a big, green, stuffed armchair next to a dark wooden coffee table but there were no other chairs in the room. Veronica sat on the edge of the bed right on top of the wool blanket. I sat next to her and it felt like there was a stiff board underneath the bedcovers. I shifted around and glanced at Veronica but she didn't seem bothered by whatever the hardness was.

"Gin and OJ okay, Matt?"

"Yes, thanks."

"What about the little lady?"

I looked at Veronica and she shook her head. I told Smitty no. A shift had occurred. Veronica not speaking for herself was a new development. I was speaking on her behalf and had never held that position before. It made me feel manly and important and mature. My love for her multiplied.

Smitty approached with my drink, his drink, and a bottle of pills. He told us they were quaaludes and recommended taking only one if we weren't too familiar with the effects. Veronica reached for one and swallowed it, washing it down with my drink. I did the same.

Veronica squeezed my hand. "Do you have any weed, Smitty?" They would be the only words she said the whole time we were there.

"Affirmative," he said with a smirk. Then he went into a kitchen drawer and took out a bag of the dirtiest weed I'd ever seen. He tossed it on Veronica's lap. "It's Hawaiian."

He was full of shit. Veronica pulled a small pack of Bambú papers out of the bag and started to roll a joint.

"Thought we could check out a few movies if you guys are into it." Neither Veronica nor I responded. "It'll take me awhile to set up the projector. I wanted to do it this morning but I was afraid my car would get towed."

Still no response from us but Smitty wasn't waiting for any cues. He started to set up a movie projector on a small table that he moved to the foot of the bed. It looked like a relic from the birth of cinema. Its electrical cord was covered in an antiquated, probably heatproof fabric that was fraying along its whole length. It felt like there was a good chance he would set the apartment ablaze once that cord was plugged into the wall.

Smitty seemed distracted by something. He abandoned the projector and left it sitting on the bed in several pieces. He went to a small cabinet between the kitchen and sleeping areas and searched through a stack of records. I couldn't make out most of them from where I sat but I did see the *Doctor Zhivago* soundtrack and *Revolver* by the Beatles. He chose something recent by Electric Light Orchestra. I didn't care for them very much and would have preferred the Beatles. But Smitty wasn't asking for anyone's musical opinions. He shuffled over to a shitty record player that was in a small plastic blue-and-white-striped suitcase. It looked like something a little kid would own.

I turned my head to face Veronica and took her in, trying to see her apart from the context of the setting. She looked dynamite that day. Put together perfectly, like a French film star. A gray skirt that was sexy but not too short, with simple gray stockings underneath. A black sweater over a white button-down shirt. She had already taken off the purple scarf, her black beret, and the big black sunglasses she wore "because it feels like too much exposure to have people staring into my eyes all day." I wouldn't blame anyone from staring into her eyes. They were intelligent eyes full of mystery and intensity. But real and honest, nothing fake. No deception.

Seeing her so composed and beautiful made me proud. And it made me want to get the fuck out of this place and take her somewhere special. The Conservatory Garden in Central Park, or the benches we liked that overlooked the East River. I wanted to stand up and tell her, *Let's go, I want to take you somewhere nice.* But I just sat there.

Veronica lit the joint. ELO started spinning on the turntable; the record scratched and skipped and then settled into a song I didn't like. Smitty went back to work on the projector. His hands were shaky and sweaty and it took him a long time to assemble the ancient machine. He had to keep wiping his hands on his pants and then he'd pause and take a few deep, wheezy breaths. There was a little bubble of white foam in one corner of his mouth. If he didn't disgust me so much, I might have felt sorry for him.

twenty-five

I didn't have the heart to disappoint Lou. I went to the diner and got the keys. I was hoping Ciro would be suspicious and catch on to what was happening but he didn't question me at all. I had the keys in my hand and walked to the parking lot. I kept telling myself that if I just went slow it would all be okay. I mean, even little old ladies drove cars, and if they could do it, how hard could it be?

I found the van to be a lot more sensitive than I'd expected. I lurched forward in little bursts and jolts as I rode the brake and pulled out of the lot. It reminded me of the way Lou had been moving while he rummaged through his kitchen.

I was very nervous . . . terrified, really; mouth dry and heart racing, white-knuckling the steering wheel. I was grateful the gin and Coke was disgusting because I couldn't imagine doing this buzzed or drunk, though if I had a few more sips maybe I would have been more calm and confident.

At the first traffic light I came quite close to rear-ending a screaming-yellow VW Bug that hesitated when the light changed quick from yellow to red. I stomped the brakes and my chest slammed into the wheel. It hurt and I would have a big bruise.

I kept fiddling with the mirrors and wasn't sure what I was supposed to be seeing when I looked into them. I couldn't get the viewing angles to make proper sense and the concept of making life-and-death decisions based on reflections in a mirror was way too risky for me. I chose not to use the mirrors at all and instead kept glancing over my shoulders every few seconds to see what was going on behind me.

The two blocks from the parking lot to my building stretched out in front of me like the Trans-Siberian Railway. It was overwhelming. Convinced that a collision was imminent, I obeyed my instincts and drove very slowly. So slowly that every driver who wound up behind me honked their horn without mercy, shouting and cursing as they passed. An old man puffing a cigar slapped the front of the van because I blocked half the crosswalk. I didn't take it personal; I just didn't want to kill anyone.

It took awhile but miraculously I arrived in front of our building without major injury or calamity. I exercised the utmost care as I shifted the transmission from D into P, stepped on the emergency brake, and turned off the ignition. I climbed out of the van and vowed not to get back behind the wheel. Lou would have to break his no-driving rule or he'd have to pay Rogelio or maybe even get Rachel out of the bedroom and have her do it. Any of the above was fine with me. I was done with driving.

I was hoping Lou would be waiting in the lobby with Rogelio and the amp sitting on a dolly, ready to go. Then the four of us, including Freddy the doorman, would hoist the thing up into the van. Freddy rushed outside to tell the driver of the van to move it and was surprised to find it was me holding the keys. I didn't see Lou anywhere so I had to explain our plan to Freddy. He said he'd be happy to help but that the van could only stay out front for ten minutes max and I should hurry.

I went up to Lou's apartment hoping to god I wouldn't run into my mother. Rachel was sitting on a cushion on the floor and Lou was laying prone with his head in her lap. Rachel's Adam's apple was protruding from her throat. I had never noticed it before. Lou had an unplugged red electric guitar cradled in his arms. He strummed some chords as Rachel stroked his head. The obscenely huge amplifier hadn't moved an inch.

Rachel looked happy. Lou wasn't singing but the tune he played was a serenade to his lady. She was the first to see me.

"Hi, Tim," she said quietly, then looked back down at her lover.

Lou kept playing and didn't turn my way. I didn't know what to do. I felt like I was intruding on something private and intimate. I just stood there in the doorway waiting for him to finish but his song went on and on. I had no choice but to interrupt.

"Lou?" He kept on strumming so I spoke up a little louder. "Hey, Lou." Still nothing. I shouted: "LOU!"

That got his attention. He stopped playing but didn't move. His eyes were peering up at the ceiling as he spoke: "I know you're there, Tim, but, as I assume you can see, I'm in the middle of something very important and I don't take kindly to being interrupted at times like this."

Rachel was looking down at him, stroking his hair.

"I'm sorry, Lou . . . it's just that . . . I have the van out front and I can only keep it there for a few minutes."

"Okay, there's the amp, did you get a dolly?"

"No, you said you would get the dolly."

"No, Tim, I told you Rogelio has a dolly. Christ, he probably has several, being that he is the superintendent of a large Manhattan apartment building. I said you should ask him if we can borrow one and if he could give us a hand getting the amp out of my house and into the van. That's what I said, Tim." Then he turned his head and looked right at me. "So unless one of us is fucking Hercules in disguise, you're gonna need a dolly to get the thing downstairs."

I went to the basement and found Rogelio. He gave me a dolly to use but said he was too busy to help us with the amplifier. Back upstairs I relayed this info to Lou, who had now sprung to life.

"Rachel can help us. She's strong. Aren't you, baby?"

"I have my moments." A Mona Lisa smile as she said it. She had cleaned up the smudged mascara and reapplied it neatly. But the bluish stubble of her beard was coming through her flesh-colored make-up. It didn't seem to bother her but I'm sure it was a constant challenge to keep it concealed as much as possible.

I could see why he liked her. She was an innately kind person with a soothing presence; very easy to be around. Except today she was wearing an excessive amount of a sharp, sweet perfume that smelled like clove. It didn't agree with me.

Lou played the role of foreman and began barking out instructions to me and Rachel. The first step was to get the amp onto the dolly. Lou offered no physical assistance as we struggled to haul it onto the set of wheels. It was very hard to do this. And it hurt. The amp was somehow even heavier than it appeared.

Rachel was indeed strong. Her hands were smooth and fleshy and were bigger than mine or Lou's, though not by much. They were not really masculine hands nor were they truly feminine. They fit who she was perfectly.

"Excellent, kids! Very well done. The worst is over. Let's get it downstairs!" Lou exclaimed as we began to push the load into the hallway and onto the elevator. He kissed Rachel on the lips as we descended.

I tried to give them privacy and just faced the door with the two of them behind me.

Right before the door opened to the lobby he said to her: "I'm sorry. Please forgive me."

She didn't reply.

We pushed the amp through to the front of the building with Lou still calling the shots but not lifting a finger. Rachel, Freddy, and I struggled to get it up off the dolly and into the back of the van.

"Use your legs!" Lou kept shouting, though I didn't know what he meant by that.

Freddy was groaning and huffing under the weight of the thing. A slight, bookish-looking guy with thick-lensed glasses and bad skin, Freddy was the weakest of our crew and his end of the amp kept sagging. Rachel was the most stoic and maintained her poise and grace throughout the ordeal. She never questioned why Lou wasn't helping us, like she somehow understood that it was better this way. I didn't understand and I resented doing it without him and having to listen to his orders.

"Heave . . . ho . . . heave . . . ho . . ." Lou was the slaveship drummer pounding out the beat as the chained rowers sweated to reach ramming speed.

We got it up and slid it into place in the van's cargo hold. Freddy was pale and looked like he was about to keel over. Rachel said I was a strong young man and gave me a kiss on the cheek. I felt a slight scrape from her stubble.

Lou took a small piece of paper from his pocket and pointed out to me what he'd written down. "Okay. Here's where you're going and here's the total price. That's what you're collecting. In cash. No checks."

So Lou was not driving or even coming with me. Neither was Rachel, who had already run back inside. I was to do it all alone. He handed over the slip of paper.

"Ask for Al when you get there. Him and his guys'll unload it for you. Make sure he gives you all the money. Don't let him haggle you, it's already been negotiated so don't take a penny less. And don't listen to any cockamamy bullshit sob story about why he's short or when he can get us the rest."

I was to meet Al at an address on the West Side across from the pier on 48th Street. In miles it wasn't so great a distance but I'd have to traverse the entire width of Manhattan through the heart of Midtown at the height of the evening rush hour. It was an insane prospect.

"Lou . . . I really don't think I should be doing this."

"Nonsense, Tim. Nonsense. I am 100 percent certain beyond a shadow of a doubt that you will successfully complete this mission. Don't fall for any of Al's pathetic cripple routines. He'll try and hustle you, play on your sympathies . . . but just stick to your guns and tell him you are on strict orders from me. I gotta go."

He slapped me hard between my shoulder blades and disappeared back into the building. I felt trapped and claustrophobic. I didn't have the strength or the will to confront and refuse him. And it wasn't because I was afraid of him, I really wasn't. I guess I just really wanted him to like me. I hadn't even heard any of his music (that's not true, I had heard one of his songs a few times) outside of the droning-feedback massacre of sound. Still, I was enchanted by him, bewitched and under his spell. He mesmerized me. When I was with him it was like being in another world altogether. Like time had slowed to a stop and I was oblivious to anything else going on in my life or in the world at large.

I couldn't let him down, yet I was sure that the crosstown journey would end in disaster. I would be fired by Ciro for crashing the van—assuming I survived the accident—and I'd owe him money for the damages; I'd be arrested for driving recklessly without a license and would have to call my mother to bail me out 'cause, god knows, Lou was not going to do it. I couldn't even be sure he'd answer the phone when I made the one call the police would allow me.

On top of all this, it was Friday the thirteenth! And that started to fuck with my head. The walls were closing in; my pulse quickened and my temples throbbed. My heart felt like it had swelled to fill my entire thoracic cavity. There was pain in my jaw, my left arm, and my groin. It was the beginning of a heart attack, I was sure. I was short of breath and afraid I was about to die.

I told Freddy I needed five more minutes and didn't wait for his answer. I ran into the building and pressed for the elevator.

twenty-six

She was in her bed. The curtains and shades were drawn, the room dark except for the flickering of the television. Her head was propped up high on several pillows and she sipped from a big glass of iced tea with no ice.

"Hey, Matty. How's my love today?"

"Can I ask you for a favor, Ma?"

"Of course. What can I do for you?"

"Can you drive me to West 48th Street and the West Side Highway? It's very important. Ciro said we can use his van."

"A van? What do you need a van for?"

"It's a favor for a friend. It's really important."

"Which friend? . . . Oh, Matty, I'm in no frame of mind to drive a van right now."

I was too late; she was sedated for the evening. I was hoping I could catch her before she dosed herself with whatever tranquilizer she had become partial to. She was right; absolutely in no condition to be driving.

"Why don't you take a cab, sweetheart?"

It started before I could answer. First they welled up in the corners of my eyes, at the ready, drawn and cocked though not breaking the boundary of the eyelid. But once the butterflies in my solar plexus took flight, there was no way to reverse the flow and in an instant I was sobbing out loud. Blubbering like a baby, like a fucking little boy, my face striped wet. I was an infant, a child, and a runt to boot. Humiliated and disgusted with myself.

"What is it, my darling boy? Come here." She sat upright looking very concerned and reached for me. "Let me hold you."

I couldn't allow myself to do that. The tears, the choking sobs, they were bad enough. There was no way I could sink into my mother's arms and let her hold me. I couldn't bear that. I tried to speak but the weeping was too much for my words.

"It's fine . . . I . . . I just . . . I have to . . . it's . . ." I was hiccuping and couldn't complete a sentence. It was horrible.

"Sit down, Matt. Tell me what happened." Worry enveloped her face.

I couldn't look at her. I hated myself and hated her for pitying me. I stopped trying to talk and tensed all my muscles to stifle the crying. I had to get control of myself. Had to snap out of it. This was such a defeat. I took a deep breath and glanced up at her. Relaxing my muscles, I said to her: "It's okay. I'm fine." I wiped my face.

"No. You're not fine. You're scaring me. Where do you need to go? Why is it upsetting you so much? I'm gonna call your boss."

"Please don't. It's okay. He has nothing to do with it."

I felt bad that I asked her in the first place and was sorry I got her so worried and confused. I had to cut the cord and get away. I had to get downstairs and into the van. I had no choice but to drive the fucking thing crosstown. The hell with it. Whatever was going to happen was going to happen. But I had to get out of there. Anything was better than this.

My mind raced to concoct a lie that would allay her fears and allow me to get downstairs without her calling Ciro and asking him questions. I went into a song-and-dance about how the favor I was asking her for had nothing at all to do with my tears. I confessed that I was missing my father lately and the last few days especially. This could not have been further from the truth but it was a convenient excuse that was there for the taking. I went on to tell her that my friend was a musician who was selling an amplifier and she needed someone to drive it crosstown but it was fine if it waited till tomorrow when her brother would be back from Milwaukee.

She looked at me with big, sad, narcotized eyes. "You can talk to your father, you know. I'm sure wherever he is, somehow he's able to hear you."

I didn't believe this for a second. But I nodded and leaned over to give her a kiss.

"I love you, Matt."

"Love you too."

"Give me my pocketbook. It's on the chair."

I left with thirteen dollars in my hand.

twenty-seven

Traffic was awful. I barely had to step on the gas at all. I drove the crosstown distance mostly using the brake pedal and the bit of forward momentum offered by the drive setting on the van's transmission. I didn't crash and completed the first leg of the odyssey without incident. I was proud and surprised.

I pulled up to what seemed to be some type of garage. A man in eyeglasses began screaming at me for blocking his driveway. Al was a tall man with one leg, his pants altered with the empty side neatly folded and pinned just above where the knee had been. There was a crutch beneath his armpit and his long, rectangular face was tinted jaundice yellow.

Par for Lou's course, Al was not expecting me. Nobody in Lou's world outside himself ever expected anything. His whole operation was run on a whim, on impulse and the assumption that things would always go his way in the end. No coordination or pre-arrangements were needed because Lou was certain that everyone else would anticipate and understand his needs through some form of telepathic communication. It was a system that proved to be an abject failure, malfunctioning every step along the way.

I tried to explain to Al who I was, who sent me, and why I was there, but he wasn't at all interested in hearing me. His lone concern was to get my van the fuck away from his driveway. This meant parking two long blocks away because my attempt to double park on the West Side Highway was met with the wrath of the evening commuters. I locked up the van and walked back to deal with my new friend Al.

My timing was incredibly bad, my visit a terrible inconvenience, and Al was holding me personally responsible. There was disgust and disdain in every word he slung at me.

"What the fuck do you think, that I'm at every asshole's fucking disposal? . . . I don't want to hear it . . . I don't run a fuckin' clinic that's open to the public without appointment! . . . Do I have to fuckin' cater to every jerkoff, dopehead, and drug addict?"

This went on as I followed Al through his warehouse and toward his ringing telephone. I was to blame for everything wrong with his life, including the mental deficiencies of his nephew and probably also his missing leg, which I began to think was several pounds of flesh exacted by the universe for some heinous crime he'd committed against nature.

"Cuntlapping faggots!!!" he exclaimed after answering the phone only to discover that he was too late. He banged the phone down and with rage-shaking hands reached for his cigarettes. He turned to face me and took a long drag. By the time he exhaled he had calmed down a little. I once again explained to him why I was there and who sent me.

"I shoulda fuckin' known. The blind leading the fuckin' blind."

"Yeah," I said with a little chuckle.

"Well, what are you standing here for? Bring it in" was his reply.

I asked if there was anyone to help me unload.

"Yeah. You're looking at him."

I wasn't sure if he was serious or not. I didn't want to offend him so I just said, "Okay."

He looked away from me and bent his mouth into a thin, crooked grin. "Yeah, right. My numb-nuts nephew is on his lunch break." He took another deep inhale and coughed loud. "You're gonna have to wait for him if you can't bring it in by yourself." His words came out mixed with long trails of smoke.

"I can't lift it by myself," I confessed.

"Isn't it on casters?" he said, but I didn't know what he meant so I just shrugged. "The amp. It should be in a case with casters on the bottom. Little wheels."

"No, no case with wheels. We used a dolly when we brought it down from his apartment."

Al shook his head, smiling sarcastically. "Your boss does everything bass-ackward, you know that? I was supposed to get the case too. That was the deal. It's always some shit with him. That's why they call it dope . . . you know what I'm saying, right? I should send the fucking thing back."

I was happy that the verbal abuse had stopped so I agreed with him.

"Okay, pull it into my driveway and let's see what's what," he said as he walked me to the door, steady and nimble for a man on one leg.

I was able to drive the van the two blocks back to Al's pretty easily. I felt some new confidence in my driving ability and thought that maybe I had underestimated myself and what I was capable of. Al was waiting beneath the open garage doors. I got out of the van and walked around to its back doors.

Al was giving the van a good once-over. "I like your truck. What do you charge?"

"For what?"

"For hauling. I need another backup 'cause my main guy is retarded and my backup is a borderline moron. What do you charge?"

I didn't know how to answer his question. I didn't even know if I was getting paid for this at all.

Lou didn't mention money. I asked Al what he paid his regular guy as I opened up the van's rear doors.

"Depends," Al replied as he came around to look inside at the giant amplifier. He shook his head.

"I can't believe that jackoff forgot the case. Can you bring it by later?"

"Sure," I lied through my teeth.

"Course, I'm not gonna pay you extra 'cause that was part of the deal. That's his fuck-up, not mine."

"Of course," I said matter-of-factly. Al and I were on the same side now.

"Arright. Close it up and lock it. We gotta wait for my nephew." Al sighed heavy. "Let's go relax till dipshit gets here. You like root beer or Pepsi?"

"Root beer."

"I got orange too. You like orange?"

"I do. Thanks."

"Nehi, not Crush. That okay, Hopalong?"

Al had one leg but I was Hopalong.

twenty-eight

The first film Smitty showed us was of a blond Swedish-looking woman going down on a black man. The movie was silent and must have been made in the early sixties, maybe even before then. I had never seen this kind of thing on film before so at first it was a shock to my system. Veronica sat quiet between me and Smitty on the edge of the bed. She didn't comment at all on the movie. Smitty just stared at the images on the screen and sipped his drink.

It was dark. The only light in the room was the flickering from the projector bulb and the pornography on the wall. The first film ended how one would imagine it to, but despite the predictability of the conclusion it was still strange and surprising to see it actually happen. Smitty stood up and asked if I wanted another drink or if Veronica needed anything. She shook her head but I asked for another. Smitty told me to help myself as he pushed some buttons on the projector and the reel started to unwind.

I tried to grab Veronica's hand before I got up to make my drink but she subtly moved it away. I was just trying to see if she was okay. There was a distance growing between us. She didn't look at me at all during the first film, even when I tried to make eye contact with her. She did give my hand a squeeze just after the lights first went out, right before the initial image of the Swedish woman's painted face. But that was it. Now she chose to ignore me.

Smitty was using his cigarette lighter as a flashlight to examine the many small reels of smut he had in his box. I thought that the name *Smutty* would be a more fitting moniker for the man and I chuckled at this revelation. But I knew it wasn't funny and I wasn't having any fun. I realized it was the pill taking its effect.

I made my drink. I was waiting for the lights to come back on but they never did. The record reached its end, the needle quietly spinning and skipping on a groove near the spindle. Smitty lifted the arm and dropped it where the first song started. We were about to be subjected to the same dreadful ELO all over again.

twenty-nine

"Guy can build a Geiger counter out of a fuckin' coconut but they can't build a boat and go home? Come on. He don't wanna go home! He's living in paradise and fuckin' both them broads! Who'd want to go home?"

We were watching a television placed on a high shelf in Al's office. I sat in a beat-up black desk chair on wheels and sipped my second orange Nehi. Al was stretched out on a couch, his lone foot in a black sock and propped up on a pillow. His crutch was laid out on the floor next to the couch, parallel to his body. We were passing the time, waiting for Al's nephew Norman (who he called "Ab-norman, the dumbest thing on two legs") to return from his break. It was getting later and later and Al finally determined that his nephew wasn't coming back and the two of us would have to handle getting the amplifier down off the van and into his shop.

We set up a big wooden ramp from the lip of the van's cargo hold to the greasy floor of the garage.

"There's a hand truck right outside my office."

I grabbed it and wheeled it up the ramp. Then I tried to jimmy its edge underneath the amplifier, which was a lot harder than I thought it would be.

"Wait for me. I'll show you," Al said as he started to hobble his way up the ramp. But the angle of the ramp was pretty steep and halfway up Al's equilibrium started to give way. He gripped his crutch with two hands, tapping it hard against the wooden ramp and then hopping on his leg. He alternated these two movements in rapid succession, tapping (more like slamming) the crutch down onto the wood and then hopping on his leg. *Tap*, hop, *tap*, hop, *tap*, hop; pogoing himself higher up the ramp in quick spurts. It was a desperate, almost graceful display of strength and coordination; a perverted Fred Astaire number.

Just as he reached the top, the rubber tip of his crutch managed to get caught in the small gap where the ramp and the van met. The sudden stop of his forward thrust pushed him off balance. I reached for Al but was too late.

His foot slipped and his leg went flying up. His back flopped hard on the ramp, then he rolled and tumbled all the way down, landing in a violent heap on the cold concrete floor.

One of the lenses of his glasses was shattered and he had ripped a tear along the whole length of his good pant leg, exposing the white jockey shorts beneath.

"Motherfucker!!!! . . . That cocksucking shitbag!!! . . . Can't rely on any-goddamn-body!!!"

"Are you okay?" He could have broken his neck the way he fell.

"Heads up their cuntlapping faggot asses!!!" His face and neck were bright red.

I put my shoulder under his arm and tried to help him upright.

"Gimme the goddamn thing." He thrust his head toward the top of the ramp. The crutch was still lodged in the gap. It stood there straight and erect like the flag in a golf hole. Al leaned against the back of the van and I ran up the ramp to free the crutch from where it was stuck. I gave it to Al as fast as I could.

"Goddamnit to hell . . . Heads up their shit-stained asses!!!!" he screamed as he wiped the sweat off his face with a handkerchief. Suddenly he froze and his eyes went wide as they fixed on something behind me.

Norman's timing could not have been worse. To add insult to injury, the unfortunate nephew was happily stoned and sipping a milkshake as he arrived. He was a short kid, not much older than me.

"Where the fuck were you? You son of a goddamn bitch!!" Al shouted so loud, so concentrated with rage, it created a bolt of static electricity that made the left side of his thinning head of hair stand straight up.

"Wh-what's the matter, Uncle Al? What happened?" Norman responded as his buzz quickly evaporated.

"*What happened?!!!* I almost broke my ass because of you, that's what fuckin' happened." Al raised the crutch high in the air and Norman cowered and covered his head. I was sure Al was about to split it open like a watermelon.

"No! Please no, Uncle Al," Norman pleaded, sounding like a bad actor.

"Doing *your* fuckin' job!! I almost killed myself, you rotten cuntbag, *doing* your *fuckin' job!!!*" Al swung the crutch but missed by a mile. It was deliberate. He could have hit him with his eyes closed.

"No, no, no, no, no!!!" Norman squealed in a high voice, his hands still covering his head. "Please . . . no, no, no, no . . ." He was breathing heavy, hyperventilating, as he begged his uncle to spare him. He had every right to be afraid, of course, but there was something in the way he expressed his fear that made me think he was faking it.

Al took another big swing and a miss, but this time Norman fell to the floor like he'd been hit.

"No, no, no, no . . . please!!! . . . Uncle Al . . . no!!!" He continued his performance, which didn't seem to be out of mockery or disrespect to Al. I don't know what it was but I didn't believe it. There was something very Kabuki about it. Or at least what I imagined Kabuki to be like.

"Dope-smoking piece of shit . . . just like your father!" Al poked Norman in the ribs with the crutch. But it was a very gentle poke, I mean he barely touched him at all.

"Owwwwww!" Norman wailed as if he'd been shot with a bow and arrow. "Owwwww!!! No!!!!" He was curled up on the floor and started sobbing and whimpering. It was the worst acting I had ever seen. Worse than the wrestlers on Channel 9.

"Sorry, Uncle Al . . . so sorry . . . so, so sorry . . ."

"I should crack your goddamn hophead skull." Al poked him again, this time on his butt. But it might have been even lighter than the first poke. And once again Norman reacted like he'd been pierced with a red-hot iron rod.

"Owwwww! . . . Aaaaaaaahhh! . . . Nooooo! . . . I'm so sorry."

"Should shove it right up your dirty fuckin' ass, you ungrateful retard!!!"

I started to think that this was some kind of very bizarre routine and it wasn't the first time this exchange had happened between them. There was a very stilted, rehearsed quality to it.

"You want more, shitheel? 'Cause I got more."

"Noooo. Nooo, please. Please, Uncle Al . . ."

"Tell me what an asshole you are."

"I'm an asshole, Uncle Al."

"Tell me what a shitbag you are."

"I'm a shitbag, Uncle Al."

"A what?"

"An asshole shitbag."

As their play got more pathetic and grotesque, I noticed that Al had opened a gash on his leg.

"Your leg's bleeding." I was glad to interrupt the high school dramatics. Al looked at me and I pointed to his leg.

"Get me some Band-Aids, shithead!" He tapped Norman on the shoulder with the crutch.

This time Norman didn't scream bloody murder. He just sniffled, got to his feet, and walked quietly to the office.

"And the Mercurochrome!!" he shouted to his nephew. Then he held his handkerchief to the wound, peered at me, and said: "Stay away from drugs."

I nodded.

"Lemme get this under control, then we'll get the thing down and you can go."

"Take your time," I said.

Norman reappeared with a bunch of paper towels, some Band-Aids, and a bottle of hydrogen peroxide. Al cleaned and disinfected his wound and bandaged himself up while poor Norman and I got to work on the amplifier. He was incredibly strong for someone his size and we got the amp onto the hand truck and down the ramp without much trouble.

"Okay. One, two, three, four, five. And that's for you." Al counted out five hundred-dollar bills into my palm, and shoved ten singles into my shirt pocket. "You're gonna bring me the case, right?"

"Yeah, of course," I lied again. I had no intention of coming back at all.

"Tonight. Before midnight."

"Okay."

"And tell freakshow that Al said, *Go fuck yourself.*"

"I will."

"You will?"

"Yeah." I looked at the floor, then toward the office where Norman sat slumped in the desk chair picking his nose.

"You'll get fired if you do. Don't say that. Just make sure he gives you the case. I need the case. He has it but he gets so stoned that he forgets. It's always like that with him, with half of the rejects I deal with. I should send my numbnuts nephew to work for him. Two peas in a pod."

Al shook my hand, then as I climbed into the van he said, "How 'bout a Nehi for the road?" Before I could answer he shouted to Norman: "Hey! Get off your ass and get the kid an orange soda!"

Norman was now picking his teeth with the same finger that was just up his nose. He didn't even bother to turn his head toward us. "Get it yourself, old man," he said casually, the show now over.

Al looked at me and shook his head with the tiniest hint of a grin. "No respect. Kids today . . . no respect at all," he muttered as he hopped to the fridge.

thirty

The second film featured a young woman, a girl really, I doubt she was eighteen. She was in a warehouse and there were two men with her and they were both old enough to be her father. I'd rather not get into the details of what transpired in the warehouse but it was ugly and disturbing. I'm guessing it was all consensual and the actors were just pretending it wasn't. But that's really more a hope than an assumption. I didn't want to look but every time I tried to turn away I couldn't. When the two men finally bent the girl into a particularly vulnerable and humiliating pose, I had seen enough and found the will to turn my head. That's when everything in the room shifted. Or maybe it shifted a few minutes before the second movie started. I'm not so sure. I got pretty upset when I saw Smitty's hand on Veronica's leg. He was touching the stocking of her left leg and rubbing the inside of her thigh, just above the knee. Her legs were spread a little more than I think they were when we first sat down. I was feeling dizzy and light-headed. My pulse was racing and my heart beat fast. My thoughts became suspicious and paranoid. Had I been poisoned? I told myself it was the drug reaching its full effect but I didn't believe it. Maybe Smitty and Veronica were in cahoots. I touched the necklace Veronica gave me. I was afraid it would start to choke me. My mind went back to the black magic store. Of course. How stupid could I be? Veronica and her family must belong to a satanic cult, Smitty was also a member, and now they wanted to draw me into it as well. Fresh meat, new blood. Maybe they wanted to offer me up as some sort of sacrifice. They did that kind of thing, the cults, didn't they? I had heard of devil cult rituals that were practiced in the abandoned water tunnel of a heavily wooded park in Yonkers—Oscarmeyer Park, or something like that. I had been there, it was near my cousin Gregory's house. I never went in so deep but Gregory did and he saw the bloodstained stone altar and the 666's and upside-down crosses painted on the walls of the tunnel. My cousin said the stuff was painted with animals' blood, but his best friend Emil's older brother Gizzy knew some of the people in the cult and he told Emil that there was a big plan among the network of cults in New York and New Jersey to begin human sacrifices in the name of the devil and virgins would be the first to be sacrificed. The girl on the screen looked like she was about to cry and I think the fat man spit on her. Why did Veronica spread her legs even farther? Couldn't she tell what a piece of shit Smitty was? I was a virgin but Gizzy had told Emil who told Gregory it was girl virgins who would be the sacrificial lambs. Was Veronica a virgin? How could I not know the answer to this question? The girl in the movie was small-framed and narrow-hipped and the men were so much bigger than her. Smitty kissed Veronica and she put her hand on my groin but I didn't like it. It wasn't supposed to be like this. This was not how I imagined it. Did Smitty put something in my drink? Yes, I took the pill but I'd tried a quaalude before and it didn't do this. Was it LSD, and I was tripping? The cult sold drugs to fund its operations, that's what Gizzy told Emil. Was Barry the Dogfucker in the cult? That seemed like a satanic thing to do, sex with animals, sex with children, right? Did the girl in the movie get paid or was she just acting like she was being forced? Was she just acting like she was gagging and choking? Veronica's hand has gone from my groin to my hand and she pulls it to her breast. Smitty is kissing or licking or biting her neck. Veronica guides my hand up underneath her shirt and I touch her breast for the first time with no barrier between my skin and her skin but I feel no pleasure, no lust, no love. I feel only fear and I don't trust her anymore. I want to get up and leave, both of us should get the fuck out. Smitty has taken off his shirt, his sunken chest and white-paste torso give off a smell like the flame on a stove. The two men have tied the girl's ankles and wrists with extension cords. They turn her over. Veronica turns and kisses me. I feel nothing. I open my mouth and she's inside it but I'm not there. I feel like I'm in the corner of the room watching the three of us. Veronica takes off my shirt and throws it to the floor. She pulls my undershirt over my head then twists it tightly so it's thin, long, and taut like rope. She wraps it around my neck from behind, pulls me to her, and kisses me again. I look down at the hair on my chest and notice it's about the same amount that Smitty has. He's watching me. He took his hands off Veronica and though his head is facing the screen, his eyes are on us. Veronica's skin is white like cream or fancy china or snow before it gets wet. I hate ELO and will despise them forever. The cult has members of all ages and their main focus apart from the cultivation of personal power . . . Wait . . . that's what Veronica said about witchcraft. It's all witchcraft. *All of them witches.* Who said that? Yes. Their main focus apart from the cultivation of personal power was sex, perverted sex, in groups, in rituals, on an altar, in a tunnel, in the woods, or in a church-like setup in someone's house or basement—best of all would be in a real church if they could find one. Gregory and Emil scared me when they said these things. They said that dogs howled from deep in the woods, they were property of the cult, and they would be sacrificed on certain holidays, not holy days but unholy days. The day after Christmas, I think Emil said. He said they did things to kids too. Smitty was standing near the screen and part of the movie was showing on him. It was the top of the girl's head and it was almost directly on top of Smitty's head like a double exposure. She was like a toy, like a doll in the hands of the two men. Veronica put my hand under her skirt where she had rolled down the pantie part of her stocking and I felt her for the first time. Smitty lit a cigarette and something smelled like ammonia. I think I was hard but I was so scared. I was convinced people were coming and once I was unconscious they would put me in a sack, like a mailman's sack, and take me. Take us. She didn't know, did she? She couldn't be a part of it. The girl in the movie looked like she was screaming in pain. Smitty was sniffing from a little dark brown bottle. It looked like a bottle of iodine. He was only wearing underwear now and was touching himself with his head still turned away but his eyes right on us. Veronica was warm between her legs, she was wet between her legs, and I didn't love her now. Not here. I don't think she loved me. Her stockings made me feel sorry for her. Is that the same as pity? Is pity the same as compassion? Did her mom buy her the stockings? She brought my fingers inside her and pretended to like what I was doing. Okay . . . now I understood. She was acting. This was a performance for Smitty, that's what he was paying for. His legs are so thin he must have some kind of disease. I look in her eyes but it's not Veronica. She is the role she's been hired to play. I get it. So am I *me*? This is a better explanation of Veronica's motives, much better than her being a cult recruiter. But we have proven that she is a witch and has a connection to that underworld. The movie is over. I won't say how it ended. It's too repugnant. Criminal. The music is adding to my illness, the harmonies calculated to unnerve me. Veronica is naked now. Smitty's hand in his shorts moves faster. I've never been with a completely naked woman before. Girl. I am a late bloomer but the hair on my chest is almost the same as Smitty's. Stay awake, don't pass out. My pants are being pulled down. Veronica took them off me. She tightens the shirt that's twirled around my neck. It doesn't hurt and I'm not choking. It's just tight. The wheels of the projector are still spinning but there's no image, only dirty white light. Now I don't see Smitty. I don't know where he is. Veronica lies back on the bed and pulls me on top of her using the noose that's around my throat. She tightens it some more and I feel the pressure but I'm not choking. Will this be how they bring me under? Gizzy told Emil that the cult killed a baby that a junkie woman gave them in exchange for a week's worth of heroin. He said they killed the baby with a silver dagger at midnight before or after Good Friday the thirteenth. Gizzy said they cut her (the baby was a girl) from the vagina to the center of her throat and the leader—the king or high priest—ate something out of the baby's guts. Veronica bites my neck and I think I feel Smitty's breath behind my head. Like sour milk and onions. The little bottle smells like ammonia. Veronica shifts her weight, I am inside her and no longer a virgin. I can imagine how wonderful this feels. I can imagine it but I can't actually feel it. I feel something but it's not pleasure. I feel pressure and friction, I feel moisture and heat. How old was the girl in the movie? Was that her first time? Was it her first movie? My legs are thin but not as thin as Smitty's. I'm forgetting to do something. I've forgotten something. Smitty's hand is the claw of a cannibal bird. Veronica turns her head away from me. In profile she looks much younger, like a junior high class photograph. Did I see that picture? There's something I should be doing or said that I would do, what is it? If Smitty is going to stab me he should do it now while my head is buried in Veronica's shoulder. I can smell her hair now. I wasn't able to smell anything coming off her body until now. It's the one comforting thing. Because everything else is foreign and strange, even the sounds she makes are not hers. They belong to the character. Let's not forget that she is acting. We are almost finished. She will get dressed and be paid and we will go. I hope Veronica and I will start over from scratch. Not this, not what we're doing this instant, but all of it, our whole friendship. Like none of today had ever happened. How much will he pay her? Is he paying me? Smitty is wiping himself with a napkin which he then balls up and tosses on the floor. What did they pay the girl in the warehouse? Smitty has backed away, retreated into a chair to get dressed. He's drinking his drink and looks tired. Veronica has picked up on this. She holds me tight. Something shudders through her like a sob. She releases the shirt from my throat. We both wear the same runic symbols around our necks. "Let's get dressed," she whispers in my ear like a conspirator. Smitty coughs and shuts off the projector. The room goes dark but little streams of light sneak in through the window shades and I search for our clothes. I hand Veronica her shirt and stockings but she's not looking at me. Smitty is almost dressed and stares at the floor. The record hits

its last grooves and it's too quiet in the dim room. My underwear is ripped. Not from today, but because it's a very old pair. Smitty lights a cigarette and turns on a lamp. I'm not afraid anymore.

thirty-one

I left Al's garage with the cash in my pocket and a can of orange Nehi unopened on the passenger seat. I pulled out of the driveway and onto the street and made a quick right onto 54th or 55th Street. I noticed a few drops of rain on the windshield. I made a left onto busy Eleventh Avenue and drove carefully to 57th Street, where I turned east to begin the crosstown trek.

The rain changed quickly from drizzle to downpour. Huge, angry drops pounded the metal top of the van. It was loud. I couldn't hear anything but falling water. Slabs of rain dropped so thick I couldn't see the car in front of me. I leaned forward as much as I could to get a better view. I was so far forward my head was touching the glass but still I could hardly see. I slowed the van to a crawl and the rain got even louder. It sounded like the roof was being pelted with little stones, and sure enough I noticed they *were* stones! Stones of ice! The rain became big frosty chunks of hail that hit so heavy I was afraid the windshield would crack open.

I had a green light at the corner of Tenth Avenue and went forward slow and cautious. A green truck behind me started honking, rude and impatient. It made me nervous so I sped up a little bit to clear the intersection. It was a risky move considering the lack of visibility but I made it to the other side of Tenth intact. The hailstones fell bigger and bigger, and were now the size of marbles. I slowed down again. I was certain one of the stones would rip clean through the roof and into my head.

I wanted to pull over but traffic was so bad there was no opening to get out of the lane. So I crept on to Ninth Avenue and stopped at a red light. The second it turned green the same guy behind me started honking again, only this time more frantic and repetitive. I started moving but it wasn't fast enough for him and he would not let up on the horn. I stepped on the gas pedal a little more.

When I reached the other side of Ninth the hail had turned back into rain. But the intensity of the storm would not let up and the sky thundered and flashed lightning. My nerves were burned. I focused every ounce of my attention on not ramming into the car in front of me. I was doing a decent job of it but my pal behind me was relentless. He couldn't change lanes or pass me because it was too congested, so he chose to torture me instead.

He was honking his horn in the same rhythmic pattern: three quick blasts and then a long droning honk. Over and over. I would have preferred a hailstone through the skull to the drilling he was giving me. It made me nauseous and my head throbbed in pain. I stepped on the accelerator and sped up a bit more than I should have, but it still wasn't enough for him.

As I approached the Eighth Avenue intersection the light was green but the *Don't Walk* sign was flashing red. Green was about to be yellow. My first impulse was to not risk it and stop at the corner, but the beast behind me pressed his cloven hoof on his horn and left it there. The light turned yellow. Then I heard another horn either behind him or to my side, and then another, and another, and so on, multiplying like loaves and fishes. It was unbearable. I was so rattled I pressed the gas pedal to the floor. The van reacted in a big chug forward but the light turned red and I got scared so I hit the brake as hard as I could. My Nehi flew off the seat, my head snapped back, and the evil green truck rear-ended me. The impact was louder than the thunder and it sent my head into the windshield with enough force to crack the glass.

I knew I had to be injured but nothing hurt at first. I picked the Nehi off the floor and then touched it to my head to check for blood. I was expecting lots but there was none. I got out of the van with the soda in my hand.

He was so close to me I could smell the decay in his teeth. A short, swarthy man with bushy eyebrows and a wiry mustache, he wore a blue mechanic's shirt with the word *Toma* embroidered in red script over his breast pocket. I wasn't sure if it was his name or his business. He spoke with Dracula's accent and cursed me in a mix of English and his native tongue.

He spat and sputtered, swearing and screaming at me. I was afraid for him. His complexion turned red and his eyes bugged out of their sockets. Waiting for a punch in the face, I apologized. I told him I was sorry but he didn't want to hear anything I had to say. I don't think it's possible for one person to express more hatred toward another without violence.

"Sorry's not to fix my fucking truck, suckdicker! Suckdicker son of fucker whore!"

Traffic had stopped in both directions. All the car horns of the earth sounded their agreement with my new friend's opinion of me. People got out of their cars or strolled over from the sidewalk with umbrellas to assess the damage and watch the fight. Toma got angrier, shook a fist in my face, and kicked my tires. He stomped and screamed like Rumpelstiltskin arguing with an umpire. I didn't know what he wanted or what I was supposed to do. Some of the bystanders were shouting stuff too and I got even more confused.

I said I was sorry once more. Toma pushed me hard in the middle of my chest and I slipped on the slick street and almost fell down. I was pressed up against the side of the van and he was right in my face again.

"Sorry's not to fix my truck, suckdicker!"

I pulled the five hundred bucks out of my pocket and handed it over; this pacified him. He looked down at the money in his hand and stopped cursing. I took a step sideways and stumbled over someone's galoshes. My feet slid out from under me and my pants pocket got caught on the corner of the open door of the van. I landed on my ass and saw that one of my pant legs was flayed open exactly like Al's a few minutes before. A woman in a Wonder Bread raincoat helped me up and asked if I was okay.

A man with wet gray hair was saying something to me in Spanish and then Toma started talking to me at the same time. The Spanish man was holding the keys to the van in his hand, waving them at me. Then he swung the van door shut and showed me the keys again. He was mad at me too. I reached for the keys but he snatched them away and yelled at me in Spanish. I couldn't hear a thing. The storm, the horns, the shouts, they all melted together into a huge menacing roar. I was wet, I was disoriented, and my underwear showed between the flaps of my torn trousers.

So I ran.

I just ran away.

Up Eighth Avenue to 59th Street and into the park. Believe it or not, I still had the orange Nehi in my hand. Thunder shook the sky and I kept pumping my legs through Central Park. Over a little bridge, through a playground, onto one of the roads, and then down a little footpath. The path led to another little bridge but this one I passed underneath. Here I finally stopped. It was dry and I doubled over to try to slow my heart and catch my breath. I gagged on a big gulp of air and puked up a splash of orange soda.

My head hurt and I had a big lump at the top of my forehead at my hairline. It wasn't bleeding.

I guess I was lucky.

thirty-two

Lou was alone in the apartment when I arrived. There was broken glass and torn-up pages of books spread all over the floor. A small lamp looked like it had been thrown against a wall. Lou was sitting on the floor, a round space around him, clear of all debris. He was writing something in a notebook.

"Just the man I wanted to see." He seemed happy I was there but was studying me like his vision wasn't working so well. "You're wet."

Wet? No. That was too puny a word for what I was. I was Noah on the night of the fortieth day. Saturated to the bones.

"I got caught in the rain."

"Go in my room and get yourself some dry clothes. I need you to come with me to see my friend's show downtown. Rachel went to visit her mother. A girl and her mother . . . you know . . . you can't separate 'em. Can't get in the middle of that triangle. Go 'head. Go look inside. Get out of those wet clothes, you'll catch your death."

The bedroom was a much bigger mess than

the living room. There were clothes thrown everywhere and the bed was almost upside down, leaning against a wall. Most of the dresser drawers had been removed and dumped on the floor.

"Sorry 'bout the mess! It's that time of the month for milady, if you know what I mean!" Lou shouted from the living room.

I found a black T-shirt and some black jeans among the wreckage. They were clean enough for me. The freshest socks I could find were a bright purple pair that were a day or two away from holes opening up at the heels. At least I was dry.

I peered at myself in the bedroom mirror and thought I was looking at Lou for a split second. In an instant I was me again. The me who had fucked things up royally and would have to answer for a shitload of mistakes. Like I said, at least I was dry.

I went back into the living room and Lou was holding a white Fender bass guitar. "This is for you. I suck at bass."

I held it in my hands. It was big and heavy and the strings looked thick and dangerous. They made me think of the Gestapo piano-string torture/execution. A death-by-strangulation that starts with choking a victim to the edge of consciousness with the thinnest string. This is repeated string by string, eighty-eight in all, each one a little thicker than the last until the fat and final string puts an end to the poor soul's suffering.

My new bass had only four strings—a quick and merciful alternative to the Nazi baby grand. I thanked Lou for my gift.

"Don't mention it. You can leave it here for now. We gotta get downtown. Mustn't be late for the the-a-ter."

I kept waiting for him to ask about the money or the amp but he never did. Ever. Technically I still owe him five hundred bucks to this day. Maybe on some level he sensed what had happened to me and was sympathetic. I don't know . . . probably not. What I did know was that the shit would be hitting the fan very soon in my world and until it did I was more than happy to accompany him wherever he was going. Tonight it was 4th Street and Seventh Avenue.

Everyone at the little theater in the Village knew Lou. He kissed and hugged the ticket taker, the ushers, the guy selling chocolate bars, and a few other assorted people who worked there. This was all before the show began and it was all done in a hurry because the curtain was about to go up.

Only there was no curtain—the players were already onstage as the audience filed in and found seats. The actors were a man and a woman and they were in bed together. When the lights dimmed and the carnival music stopped, the couple started having loud sex under the covers. It was very physical and very funny. Naked from the waist up, they tried out a bunch of complicated positions. They were pretending to be passionate and giving it their best effort but found none of the positions satisfying. The woman eventually gave up in frustration. The man asked her what was the matter and she pointed to a corner of the room and said: "Him. He's the matter!"

A spotlight landed on a chair upon which sat a ventriloquist's dummy.

The man replied: "He's just a dummy, honey. Ignore him."

The dummy said, "Speak for yourself, buddy. Better yet, step aside and let me show you how it's done."

The audience roared and the lights went black. The actors left the stage and the stagehands moved some furniture. I glanced over at Lou and saw that he wasn't laughing at all, not even smiling. He was just staring at the stage, angry and intense.

The play was an over-the-top farce, like something you'd see on *The Carol Burnett Show.* It was a simple story about Donald and Rose, a failed stand-up comedian and his devoted wife. Donald tries his hand at being a ventriloquist and turns out to be very good at it. His act is hilarious and he gets more and more successful as the play progresses. But as this happens, the dummy replaces the ventriloquist's wife as the man's constant companion and confidant. Finally, in an act of jealous desperation, Rose smashes the dummy's head to bits with a hammer.

But she's too late; Donald has now "become" the dummy and lost all of his compassionate and loving qualities. Insisting on being called "Wendell," Donald is a cruel and heartless shell of who he once was and blames Rose for killing his best friend. The final scene takes place in a psychiatrist's office where the wife pours her heart out to Dr. Ariel Marx, who claims to be the youngest Marx brother. The shrink is played by the same actor who played the ventriloquist and the audience is left wondering if Donald, who became Wendell, has now become Dr. Marx and perhaps was Dr. Marx all along. The finale of the play has Rose straddling Dr. Marx as she says: "I left my wallet at home. Is this an acceptable form of payment, doctor?"

The doctor replies, "Don't ask me. Can't you see I'm just a dummy?"

They begin making passionate love as the audience laughs hysterically, the lights go to black, and the play ends.

The crowd of about seventy-five people stood

and applauded when the two actors took their bows. As I got to my feet to join the ovation, I looked over at Lou. Slumped in his seat, the man was devastated. Tears fell down his face and he was sobbing as quietly as he could. In between sobs he repeated to himself, "Oh . . . oh man . . ." until the applause subsided, the actors left the stage, and the house lights came back on.

I knew the show had been getting to him. Just before the scene with the shrink, Rose took her wedding and engagement rings off her fingers and threw them to the floor. When she did it, I heard Lou gasp as if someone had punched him in the gut. I had looked at him and he was staring at the stage with his mouth wide open and shaking his head in disbelief.

We were the last people to leave the theater. Lou told me he needed to "get himself together" before he could go backstage and congratulate the actors. He told me to wait for him right outside of the bathroom and to not leave under any circumstances. He was in the men's room for a very long time and I waited patiently. I was fine with waiting. I was fine with anything that kept me from confronting the inevitable.

I was in a heap of trouble. I knew I had to face

up to everything soon. Ciro was going to go apeshit on me and I would be fired and have to pay for the van. Well, my mother would have to pay for the van and she'd be upset with me and Ciro would scream at me. And eventually I would have to come clean with Lou and pay him back the five hundred bucks. It was a disaster.

When he came out of the bathroom he looked more wrecked than when he went in.

"Let's go backstage, Tim. I have to say hello. They all know I'm here. It would be very rude to not say hi."

We went down a hallway and through a narrow door. We were in the wings and I could see the set from where I stood. The stage looked much smaller from this angle. It seemed so much wider and deeper from our seats and I wondered how the actors were able to move around so freely and with so much conviction and energy in such a tiny, claustrophobic space. It made me respect them even more than I already did.

A bald man with a bullet-shaped head appeared and screamed: "Well, look at what the strays dragged in!"

Lou was happy to see the man and hugged him hard. "So good to see you, Hal. So, so good to see you." Lou was hanging onto him longer than was normal. Like a mourner at a funeral for a close relation.

Hal looked at me from over Lou's shoulder and crossed his eyes as if to say, *What's his problem?* Then he led us down a tight spiral staircase to the basement where the dressing rooms were.

As we wound our way down, we heard the voice of Wendell the dummy saying, "Is he really here! Has my long-lost friend the evil rock star graced us with his presence?"

"Yes, Donald, it is I. In what's left of my flesh," Lou said as he stepped onto the hard concrete floor of the moldy cellar.

"Donald left through the fire door, he didn't want to see you. He told me he hates your guts," said Donald, the actor, who was still in costume and makeup. He held the dummy on his arm and made the doll do all the talking.

"Tell him it's mutual," Lou replied as he tried to give the actor a hug. Donald sidestepped him and offered the dummy for Lou to embrace. Lou refused.

"I'll tell him if you give me some sugar." The dummy presented his cheek for Lou to kiss. Lou didn't like this.

"The show's over, Donald. So get off the fucking stage and show my friend and me some hospitality."

But Donald wouldn't break his character and the dummy kept talking: "The shows not over till I'm in my box for the night. Speaking of *in my box*, who's the jailbait?" The dummy raised his eyebrows up and down and rolled his eyes at me.

"None of your fuckin' business. Where's Rose? Rose!"

Lou walked past Donald and knocked on a door that had a red glitter star on it. I followed him and ignored the dummy's wolf whistles and catcalls.

"Rose!" Lou shouted with desperation as he knocked on the door.

"The dressing rooms are for performers only, bitchface." The dummy was mad.

Lou spun toward Donald and said: "One more word and I will punch your fuckin' lights out. Got it? You cheap fuckin' whore. Get yourself to the West Coast. They know what to do with soulless hacks like you. They'll put you right on *The Hollywood Squares*."

Donald and his dummy retreated into the other dressing room and closed the door behind them. Almost at the same time the actress opened her door. She was wearing a white bathrobe and her hair was wet. Out of her stage makeup she looked smaller, younger, and kinder. She was thrilled to see Lou and lunged into his arms.

"I heard you were here but I didn't believe it." She grabbed Lou tight and he squeezed her even harder. It released something in him and brought the tears and sobs once again.

"Oh, Rose. You were so brilliant, so good. It wrecked me, it really wrecked me. Just hit me so hard."

Rose was surprised at Lou's emotion. And he wouldn't let her go.

"When you took the rings off, I just . . . you have no idea. You are a genius. I am . . . like shattered . . ."

"Thank you, Lou" was all she could say. He pulled away and introduced me as his secretary. She extended her hand and shook mine firmly.

Lou just kept staring at her. "What a fuckin' performance. Just . . . just . . . I wanted to ask . . . you know . . . because you're an actress and you experience pain in imaginary ways . . . does it . . . does it . . . does it mitigate the suffering you feel in real life? . . . I would think because you're so consciously used to it and you have a perspective, an objectivity, you know? . . . There's a distance, right? . . . Does it help you in real life when everything starts to fall apart?"

Rose kissed him on his forehead. "It doesn't hurt any less, Lou."

"No, but tonight, when you took the rings off, you had to know, right?"

"Had to know what?"

"Sorry. I'm sorry. I write songs about . . . you know . . . but you . . . I'm like an actor but I'm not . . . I'm just . . . I'm sorry . . . I gotta go. Great work, my friend."

"Do you want to get a drink? We can talk if you like."

"No. I have to go, Rose. Thank you . . . Call me, please."

"I will. Thanks for coming tonight."

"Of course. It's my privilege."

On the street I felt some drizzle falling. Lou was walking up Seventh Avenue and stayed five steps ahead of me, mumbling to himself. He stepped off the curb and stuck his hand up. A cab swerved toward him. I ran to catch up and hopped in the cab after him. He wouldn't slide over in the seat and I had to climb over him. He closed the door and told the driver to take us to Washington Street.

"I need to make a stop, Tim."

"Okay."

"You'll have to wait in the cab."

"Okay."

We got to Washington Street way downtown and it started pouring again. Lou went into a building and I sat in the cab for almost an hour as the meter slowly ticked away, dime after dime after dime. I had no problem waiting.

thirty-three

It was dark when we left his building and hit the streets. We turned down Smitty's offer of a ride downtown and decided to take the bus. I don't remember why we didn't catch the subway but I think it was Veronica's decision. We avoided making eye contact and walked three blocks to the bus stop in silence. There was an ice cream truck idling at the corner of 204th Street and Broadway.

"Do you want an ice cream? My treat." She said it without looking at me.

"No thanks." I was honest. I didn't say it out of spite. I just genuinely had no appetite for ice cream or anything else. I can't say that I was angry at her or felt betrayed or double-crossed. I was feeling something but it wasn't really directed at her. Well, it was but it wasn't. It's hard to explain.

"Would you mind if I got myself one?"

"I'll get you one." I felt it was my duty. "What do you want?"

"C'mon, Matthew. You know exactly what I want."

It may have been the first and only time I ever heard her say my name. Now I know that sounds strange and it is possible that I'm wrong, but I cannot remember her saying it any other time.

I did know exactly what she wanted. I walked over to the truck's window and bought Veronica a Bomb Pop. I used the twenty-dollar bill that Smitty gave me for services rendered. The ice cream man was not happy at having to break such a large bill and he made me wait until he served three or four other people. I understood, and I was sorry. It was a lot of change to make for something that cost twenty-five cents but I wanted to get rid of the filthy twenty as soon as I could.

I unwrapped the Bomb Pop, twirled a napkin around the bottom of the stick, and handed it to Veronica. She finally looked at me and said, "Thank you." She wasn't exactly happy but she was in a much better mood than just a few minutes ago when we left Smitty's.

If you didn't know, a Bomb Pop is a red, white, and blue Popsicle shaped like a torpedo. Each color is a different flavor. Red is cherry, white is lime, and blue is raspberry for some strange reason. The colors are three separate sections but after a few minutes of sucking, they all blend into a purpley-blueish blur. This of course leaves you with bright blue lips, tongue, teeth, and hands. Which is exactly what happened to Veronica as we rode the M100 down Broadway.

With each stop the bus made, the purpler Veronica became. By the time she finished her pop, the stains were so deep I feared they would be permanent. I had seen this before though. She never failed to make a mess of it. And she didn't care what she looked like or what anybody else thought about it. I loved her for that. It was something that always made me very happy to see. But today was different. Today it was the saddest thing in the world.

We both got off near Union Square. Veronica went into a diner to use the restroom. When she came out she was clean again, all traces of blue washed away. I escorted her as far as Astor Place, where she told me it was best we parted ways. And making no future plans, we said goodbye. No kiss.

I watched her walk down St. Mark's Place until she disappeared into the wilds of Alphabet City.

I headed north on Third Avenue. It was about a three-mile walk to my house and I don't recall any of it. The next thing I remember is knocking on Lou's door.

thirty-four

I heard the music before I got to his door. It was open just a sliver so I pushed it a little wider. He was on the rug playing an acoustic guitar. I had never seen him with anything but an electric. He played a very simple riff over and over again. Two chords. It was hypnotic—concentrated and sad.

And so was he.

He didn't notice me for about thirty seconds because his head was bent and cocked at an odd angle down toward the gaping orifice of the instrument. There was a photograph and a red tank top at his feet. He may have been staring at either one of them. Or both. A bottle of Johnnie Walker Black sat a little to his right.

He looked up and saw me in the doorway. He didn't stop what he was doing but gave enough of a nod to say I was welcome to come in. I didn't want to interrupt him but I didn't want to leave. I wanted to stay inside of that moment with him . . . inside the quiet. It felt right. It almost felt good. I sat on the floor across from him. I didn't feel like a guest. I belonged there. It was mine as much as his that day.

"I'm composing a symphony, Tim. It's something I think I will be very proud of."

He kept on strumming the two chords of his song. It was sparse, stark, and bare, but I'm sure he was hearing much, much more than what was coming out of his guitar.

"It's a symphonic suite. Very formal and structured with scrupulous discipline. I'm putting everything I have into this one. Everything I have and everything I can get . . . The New York Philharmonic strings, the Mormon Tabernacle Choir—no, fuck the Mormons . . . I'd rather the Vienna Boys." He glanced at me. "I want the middle part to sound like the last day of heaven . . . celestial voices, violins, and cellos. I love cellos. The cello is the musical instrument that resembles the human voice more than any other."

He stared at the photo. As my eyes got used to the room's dim light, I could see it was a picture of him and Rachel. He was sitting on her lap and her arms were wrapped around him in a very protective way. She was wearing the same red tank top that was on the floor in front of him.

"Tim me boy, this will be the first rock song to change water into wine, feed the multitudes, and raise the dead from their tombs."

This last statement made him chuckle.

"And as the middle part hits its coda, God reaches down with His purple and His finger and grabs Adam right by the apple. Then the words start coming. And now I'm the coldest motherfucker who ever walked a block in Harlem mid-December. Bobby Sledge, a.k.a. Bobby Rikers, carried a straight razor in his boot. Every time he went to the toilet he'd dip the blade into the bowl before he flushed whatever it was that came out of him. So the blade was constantly contaminated with all kinds of breeding bacteria, amoebas, parasites, and boogeymen. Woe unto she who got a bit of Bobby's blade."

Lou stopped playing the guitar, took a big swig of Scotch, and lit a cigarette. He coughed five or six times after the first long drag and hacked up something nasty into a tissue. Then he stuck the smoking ciggy back into his mouth and resumed his riff.

"And Bobby's gonna just tell the truth, man, right in the middle of the fuckin' church. He's gonna lay out all of the cold, heartless, pitiless reality of this gutter we call life on earth."

Another pause in the music as he took a long pull on his cigarette.

"And then, just as sudden as it started, it changes; *bang!* And now it's 1957 and we're on a street corner in the Bronx in the middle of the night and Dion and the Belmonts are serenading all our sisters and our mothers and our lovers. Shit, maybe I'll ask Dion to do it himself, sing a few bars or a chorus. That would be very cool. You like Dion, Tim?"

"I like 'The Wanderer.'"

This made Lou laugh. "You got good taste, kid. Maybe I'll get you instead of Dion."

He stopped talking and kept playing for a long time. It seemed like it would go on this way forever. Then he started singing: "*Love has gone away, and there's no one here now . . .*"

He repeated these lines over and over. I'd never heard his voice sound that way before. It was a delicate, fragile, wounded voice and it echoed off the thick white of the walls. Then he added: "*Took the rings off my fingers . . .*"

The last phrase broke him. He kept strumming but stopped singing. He didn't cry or sob audibly but the tears fell on his hands and strings.

I reached for his cigarettes without asking. It was both deliberate and unconscious and I had never done it before. He caught me out of the corner of his eye but didn't question my being so bold. I think it pleased him, though his face was so full of misery I can't say for sure. The fight and ferocity had left him. So had the cruelty and viciousness he could access in an instant. The child was in his eyes; I felt like his older brother.

The three silver rings he wore on his fingers were gone. And so was Rachel. I didn't have to ask. The song was proof beyond a reasonable doubt. She was gone and he would be too. I couldn't imagine him remaining in the home they shared. I don't think he liked being alone yet there weren't many people he liked being with. Knowing this made me feel special.

He changed the rhythm of the song; the pace quickened and he started singing again. There was a new tension in his voice as he repeated the phrases about his lost love.

After several refrains he began to chant: "*Come on and slip away . . .*"

I wasn't sure what that meant. Did it mean to die? Did it mean to withdraw from the world and all its heartbreak and violence? Did it mean to get as high, as numb, as anesthetized as possible?

He stopped his song. It was abrupt like the needle being yanked off a record. His hands and arms went slack over the guitar like he was cradling it. Like he was shielding it from all the evil in the world.

He lifted his head, the tears stopped. I had a strong desire to talk to him about Veronica but I knew I couldn't. Not because this was a bad time, I just felt in my bones that it wasn't in the cards and I'd never be able to bring it up with him.

But just as soon as this thought dissolved into

the air of the room, Lou turned to me and said: "Why didn't you tell me your girlfriend's pregnant?"

Bang.

I will never know for sure if Veronica was pregnant at that exact moment he mentioned it, but it was a possibility, one that I hadn't entertained, though certainly possible . . . So why did he say that? . . . Did he know something I didn't? And if so, how? . . . Did he tap into some strange clairvoyant energy that became accessible to him because of the deep despair that swallowed his mind, cracking open some kind of psychic window? Or was it not true at all? . . . Just some out-of-the-blue random statement, a spurt out of a brain soaked with Scotch, speed, and sorrow? I will never know . . . and I didn't know how to answer.

"What?" was all I could handle saying to him.

"Why didn't you tell me your girlfriend's pregnant?" He repeated it without breaking his gaze.

"That's not possible," I lied.

"Did something happen?"

"No. Nothing happened at all." Another lie. What he was saying scared me.

"I'm sorry, Tim. I don't know why I would say such a thing. I'm in a bad way, my friend."

"It's okay."

"I think I need to sleep."

I took that as my cue and stood.

"You can stay. I'm going inside to lie down. You can stay in here. We got a TV."

I hadn't noticed it before but there was a brand-new RCA color set in the corner of the room.

"Make yourself at home." He got up and walked to the bedroom.

I turned on the TV. It came on quick and loud. I felt the noise was inappropriate so I turned the volume all the way down. On the screen was an old black-and-white movie. A bunch of hobos were sitting by a fire near the railroad tracks. One of them was cooking something in a big cauldron, the others passed a bottle of wine. The cook had big, sad eyes and was either singing or praying as he stirred the pot.

Lou was watching from the corridor. "Oh, that's a good one. What's his name? That actor? I love him."

"I don't know."

"You can put the sound up, it won't bother me." Then he reached in his pocket and tossed me a key chained to a rabbit's foot that had been dyed blue. "If you need to go, lock up and leave the key downstairs."

I put the sound up. The bum was singing a church song, a gospel song about the heaven that waits and the god who forgives.

Lou was still watching. "Mulligan stew," he said. "What?"

"That's what he's cooking. Mulligan stew. The hobos put whatever they can find into the pot and the mulligan mixer makes it into a stew. It's gotta have some kind of meat or chicken parts, though, or at least an organ, to be a mulligan. Without meat it's just called beggar's stew. I had some mulligan once, just outside of Pittsburgh. I was skeptical but it was delicious as fuck. Surprised the shit out of me. Like when I busted my left pinkie."

"What?" I couldn't follow his train of thought.

"Limitations, man. I couldn't use my pinkie for four months. I didn't think I was gonna be able to play guitar till it healed but I wound up writing three dozen tunes I'd never have come up with if I hadn't lost the use of the pinkie."

I didn't see the connection he was making yet it still made sense somehow.

"It's like when you bust a string on the guitar and you see all these different possibilities you never saw before on the fretboard."

Lou walked into the bedroom, closed the door, then opened it and walked back to the living room. He stood right over me.

"One more thing before I forget . . ."

Here it comes. I knew it. He was going to ask

about the money. I was about to apologize and promise him I would somehow repay him, but before I could open my mouth he mussed up my hair and said: "Your bass is in the closet. Make sure you take it with you." Then he turned and went back down the corridor.

"Thanks, Lou."

"Thank *you*, *Matthew*. Use it in good health."

The stress on my real name was unmistakable. I heard him giggle behind his bedroom door, the bastard.

I watched the rest of the movie and let myself out.

thirty-five

Veronica and I hadn't been in touch since we parted at Astor Place. I called her a few times but she was never home and any message I left went unreturned. More disturbing was the fact that she hadn't returned to school. I went down to her building on several occasions and waited across the street for a few hours but never saw her come or go. I didn't have the courage to ring the bell which made me question if I really wanted to see her at all. But why else would I have been standing outside her house?

The truth was I missed her terribly. I felt so close to her, closer than I've ever felt to anyone, and at the same time I felt so far away. I wanted to see her every day for the rest of my life and I wanted to never see her again as long as I lived.

But mostly I wanted to see her. Be near her. Next to her. That's all. That would have been enough. I'd have been happy not saying any words at all.

The last day I stood watch, her building seemed different to me. I was suddenly struck by its extreme rectangularity. Looking up toward the roof from my post across the street, it loomed before me, long, black, and suffocating. It was only a five-story structure but the two buildings that flanked it were less than half its size. The two skinny trees in front were equidistant from the doorway, which was dead center, giving the whole picture a cold and formal frame. Something about the symmetry disturbed me. It was as if the building was alive and breathing and staring right at me. It made me feel like it didn't want me there.

That same day I saw Sanoo come out of a taxi and go into the building carrying a big bag of groceries. I only watched her for thirty seconds or so but the difference between her and her sister was blatant and clear. Veronica's face was both open and mysterious and her smiles came unexpected, like a warm afternoon sun in February. At twenty-one, Sanoo's face had already set into a hardness that expected the worst in people, with a readiness to attack at the slightest provocation. She frightened me. There was no approaching her at all.

After three weeks of radio silence, I asked our history teacher Mr. Gorman if Veronica had switched schools. I liked Mr. Gorman and he liked Veronica. He called her "Countess," with the accent on the second syllable. I think the nickname pleased her.

It was right after the 3:10 dismissal bell and Mr. Gorman was rushing out the front entrance. My question took him off guard but he didn't break stride or even look me in the eye. He seemed very uncomfortable with what I asked him.

"I'm sorry, Matthew . . . ummmm . . . I don't . . . I don't have anything to tell you." He patted my shoulder and darted into the street like he couldn't get away from me fast enough.

A little orange car was double parked at the corner. Mr. Gorman's wife got out of the driver's seat and walked around to the passenger side as Mr. Gorman replaced her behind the wheel. He looked at me through the window and after a strange wave, he drove off.

This did not bode well.

I never figured out how my mother knew before I did. I assumed it was through the school but I am not 100 percent certain. She broke the news to me very gently, with a lot of compassion. I can't say I went into immediate sorrow or grief or horror or shock.

The first feeling I remember was revulsion: a sickness . . . disgust. There was something obscene, something profane about the act itself. I felt it would have been better left a secret or an ambiguous "natural causes," even if it was a lie and there was nothing at all natural about a seventeen-year-old girl being dead.

Then I realized that the disgust I felt was toward my mother. Her knowledge of what Veronica chose to do to herself was an invasion of privacy. Both Veronica's and mine. I didn't want to share that space with anyone, least of all my mother. It was mine, and mine alone, because she was dead and the dead have no right to privacy. The dead have nothing. They *are* nothing. They're gone.

My mother of course did not go into any detail about the actual method my love had chosen. Knowing Veronica the way I did, I narrowed it down to three possibilities:

1) Slit wrists in the bathtub. The two of us once spoke about the ancient Roman way, which was said to be peaceful and painless, although the slashing part couldn't possibly be painless and the peace would only come after enduring the violence of the slicing. We also discussed how this method was not very peaceful to the person finding the bloody mess of a corpse submerged in all the sickly pink water and the tiles and shower curtains splattered in garish red. Suicide is always an act between two people, isn't it? The one committing it and the one who discovers it. I wondered how much she had considered that before doing what she did.

2) Pill overdose. A more likely choice for Veronica. Far more peaceful and painless than wrist-slitting but a long waiting period between the ingestion of the agents and the onset of the incapacitating effects needed to shut down one's life-sustaining systems. The gap of time was a stumbling block for me because it required a high degree of patience, a virtue I would not under normal circumstances attribute to Veronica. So unless she was in some inspired state of beatific grace, I find it hard to imagine she'd summon enough forbearance to sit tight until the drugs were digested and assimilated into her veins and organs. Yet in blatant disregard of the above argument, I have made the choice to acknowledge this mode of self-destruction as her final act of will. I have convinced myself this is how it happened because I do not want to accept the abominable reality of what she most likely did to herself. Which not coincidently leads us to:

3) Hanging by the neck until she's dead, dead, dead. Veronica once commented that the second-floor fire escape behind her building would make an excellent and effective gallows.

The day after I received the news I went down to her building, rang all the bells (except for hers), and was buzzed in. I walked past the trash bins, through the rear door, and into the backyard. There was no evidence of a crime scene. (It was technically a crime, wasn't it?) I sat down on a rotted old picnic table and started to write her a letter. I didn't look up.

thirty-six

My mother thought it might be a good idea for us to get out of town for a while. She first suggested buying plane tickets and heading off to Paris or Rome but I talked her out of going anywhere too far. So we settled on a tour of New England. My mother wasn't up for driving and she felt a train or bus would be inconvenient, so she hired an older cousin of mine to drive us in his '68 Charger.

Connie (short for Constantin) was five years older than me and we weren't close at all. He was a short, squat fellow with thick-framed eyeglasses and long, poorly cut black hair. And he had terrible skin, pockmarked and pimpled.

I thought it was a bad idea to have Connie join us on the trip. He certainly wasn't the brightest bulb on the family tree and he had a reputation for being clumsy, lazy, and dishonest; a winning combination for sure. Connie's own mother fired him from the family restaurant in Astoria for stealing fish and cheese and selling it to other restaurants in the neighborhood. One of which was owned by another relative. Yes, we were in great hands for sure.

The plan was to head straight to Boston. Connie was excited because he had always wanted to see the Liberty Bell. I didn't have the heart to tell him it was three hundred miles in the opposite direction.

We left Manhattan at five thirty in the morning on a Friday. My mother asked Connie's permission to sit with me in the backseat. He was fine with it. She was really worried about me and held my hand for most of the trip. Connie's saving grace was that he didn't talk much, so after about two hours on the road, Mom and I fell asleep for a long time. Long enough for Connie to reach Boston, where his keen navigational skills failed him. He couldn't figure out what exit to get off the freeway and he missed the city entirely. When my mother and I woke up we were thirty miles north of Boston in Salem, Massachusetts.

I took this as a very bad sign but didn't want to say anything to my mother. It would have been useless to say anything to Connie, who wanted to find the factory where they made the cigarettes. He was hoping for free samples, once again astounding me with his peerless geographic knowledge.

We went into a little restaurant for breakfast. I had a peanut butter and jelly sandwich on the ride up (Connie had three) so I wasn't hungry and ordered just a cup of tea. Connie was a little hungry so he ordered three fried eggs with bacon, sausage, ham, potatoes, toast, and a chocolate milkshake. My mother asked for coffee and cinnamon toast.

"We don't serve it," said our waitress Molly, who wore a name tag in the shape of a conical witch hat.

My mother tried to politely explain what cinnamon toast was, but Molly the Witch cut her off: "I know what it is, lady, we just don't serve it."

My mother gave up: "I guess I'll just have some corn flakes then."

"It's bread, cinnamon, sugar, and butter. You don't have those four things?" I spoke up in my mother's defense.

My mother turned toward me surprised.

"It's not a matter of whether or not we have the ingredients, it's a matter of what's on the menu and what the chef—"

"Are you fucking stupid or just a nasty bitch?" I really let her have it.

"Matthew!!" My mother was mortified.

"I think it's best if you people leave," Molly said. She scooped up the menus and walked into the kitchen. My mother gave me a look that was more confused than angry. Then she got up and followed Molly into the kitchen.

"She deserved it, Matt. Good for you," Connie

said as he nodded his head and searched his pockets. "Want a Seconal?"

I shook my head.

My mother returned and didn't say a word to me. It was like it never happened. A few minutes later Molly brought the tea, coffee, and milkshake. She didn't say a word either.

"I'm sorry, ma'am." I meant it too.

"We all have our days," Molly replied without looking at me.

My mother's breakfast was a disaster. Way too much sugar, not enough cinnamon, and saturated in butter. She ate it without a complaint. Connie (short for *connoisseur*) ate his morning meal in giant gulps and slurps. I began feeling sick to my stomach and went to the bathroom. Not to throw up but to get as far away from my dear cousin as I could without leaving my mother abandoned.

After breakfast my mother got directions to the only standing structure left in Salem with a direct link to the witchcraft trials. In a display of great originality and imagination, the building is called "The Witch House." Which would be dumb enough except for the fact that no witch ever lived there.

The Witch House had been the home of Judge Jonathan Corwin, who resided there from 1675 until his death in 1718. Judge Corwin had the distinct honor of sending nineteen innocent people accused of practicing witchcraft to the gallows. He also condemned the lucky Giles Corey to "death by pressing." This involved Mr. Corey being placed under a board which was weighted down with heavy stones added one at a time. It took the poor soul two whole days to die.

After accomplishing the heroic feat of ridding Salem of its witches, the Honorable Judge Corwin was appointed to the Massachusetts Supreme Court. We were granted the distinct privilege of visiting the home of this paragon of justice and virtue.

The house was made of a sinister-looking gray-black wood and stood three stories tall. There were only three windows on the entire side of the house that faced the street. They were abnormally small like teeth and eyes. They unsettled me. I didn't want to go inside but my mother had her arm inside mine and I was reluctant to break away from her. Connie was doing a bad impression of the Wicked Witch of the West, cackling "Heh-heh-heh, my pretty" as we entered through the gift shop.

The house was dark inside, the small windows didn't allow much light. The floorboards creaked and the air was thick with the scent of old wood, mildew, and wet paper. Karol, our tour guide, wore a black seventeenth-century getup with breeches, stockings, garters, and a Pilgrim hat. His Polish-accented English completed the period costume. Karol showed us a glass case that displayed an amulet containing skull moss (actual moss that grew on a dead human skull) that was used to ward off witchcraft. The amulet did not belong to the Corwin family but was found in the basement of a demolished church. Also in the case was a small, white cloth doll, crudely made in the image of a little girl. There were two stitched X's where its eyes should have been and it wore no specific articles of clothing. No genitalia were represented, thank god, but it was obscene just the same. Karol said it was a *poppet* and was used by witches to cast spells. It, too, had come from somewhere other than this house.

I was sure that some evil energy drove me to this place, leading me into the presence of dark forces. Was I to be forever damned, cursed, and doomed? I was dizzy and couldn't think straight. Karol began leading us up a narrow set of stairs and I felt the walls closing in. I knew this trip was a stupid fucking idea. Vomit churned in my gut, my mouth salivating, my heart pounding. I needed to get out or I was going to puke and pass out. I pulled on my mother's arm and everything went black.

Next thing I remember is sitting on a patch of grass outside the Witch House. Connie was standing above me with his head cocked at a weird angle. "Are you back, Dorothy?" He thought he was very funny.

Karol was next to Connie, his big black hat in his hands, a cigarette in his mouth. My mother kneeled down and gave me sips of water from a black *Salem, Mass* mug. I told her I wanted to get in the car and drive the hell away from there.

I wanted to go home.

I wanted to see Lou.

thirty-seven

I stood at his doorway wearing the clothes he gave me. I thought he would get a kick out of that. I knocked. Nothing. I tried knocking three more times. On the fourth there was still no answer and I started to worry. In my pocket was his key and the foot of the poor blue rabbit. Now that I think about it, it must have been Rachel's key. I let myself into the apartment.

The living room was empty. There was never a lot of stuff in the place before but now there was none: Lou had moved out. And I know it wasn't him who packed up the joint and hauled everything out. There was no way he would have done such a thorough job. Besides being empty, the place was also spotless. And that just wasn't in his nature.

Even the kitchen was empty. The cupboards, the drawers, the refrigerator: nothing. The bathroom too. I was sure that something had to have been left behind somewhere. It just seemed too strange that not even the smallest trace of the man remained.

In the bedroom my suspicions were proven correct. On the wall between the two windows were about twenty lines of lyrics or poetry scrawled in red ink. At the foot of the wall a thick red marker sat quiet on the floor.

I read his words carefully and silently. They were frightening and beautiful at the same time. I know they came from a place of deep pain, because that was how I left him. Even with his tale of mulligan stew and the game he played with my name, I knew he was suffering. That's why I was worried for him.

Maybe this was it. The last words the world would ever get from the man.

I started to recite the lines out loud. The first run-through I was quiet and slow but then I started over from the beginning. I picked up the volume and the pace and the second reading was much better. The third time was even louder and faster and I tried to put myself in his shoes (I was already wearing his pants and shirt) and feel whatever it was that he'd been feeling at the time.

By the fifth recitation I was screaming, scraping my throat raw, trying to put every ounce of what I was feeling (what *he* was feeling) into the performance. I was punching and kicking the air for punctuation and it felt like my body was doing these things independent of any commands from my brain. On the last word I kicked the air so hard and so high, I landed flat on my back and my head smashed against the hardwood floor.

It was dark when I woke up and I didn't know where I was. My head was throbbing and my back ached. Slowly it all came back to me and I remembered I was in Lou's empty bedroom. As I got to my feet, the room swayed a little. I didn't feel well. I wasn't sure if there was still electricity in the place so I flipped the switch. The bare bulb in the ceiling fixture lit up the room so bright it was brutal.

I felt that it was my duty to transcribe what was on the wall for posterity. I figured that no copy of the piece existed anywhere and it was sure to be whitewashed in a day or so. I searched the apartment again. There had to be something, a book, a menu, a bill, a piece of cardboard, something I could use to preserve what may have been Lou's last words. The task had fallen upon me; I was to be keeper of those final words.

There was a small cupboard in the kitchen, high above the refrigerator. I had missed it on first inspection. I had to climb on top of the stove to reach it. There was no paper inside, nothing to write on, nothing at all except a half-empty bottle of gin. I reached for it cautiously, climbed off the stove with care, and took the bottle back to the bedroom. I toasted the scripture on the wall, bid Lou farewell, and took a big swig. This I knew was stupid because I needed to go up to my apartment and find some paper. Gin really stinks up the breath and my mother would smell it and get upset and scared for me. And I was already feeling sick and still a little dizzy.

I took an even bigger swig. It burned but it made me happy. I sat on the floor, another big swallow. I thought about the time he took me to the bar and officially dubbed me Tim. I hated the name but accepted it because I felt neither of us had any choice in the matter. I underestimated you. Cheers. One more pull from your bottle.

I started on my left forearm. That would be the most logical place since I'm right-handed. It tickled at first but became more and more pleasurable as my skin got used to the sensations. The first line read: *They tied his arms behind his back to teach him how to swim.*

I rotated my arm slightly and continued on the soft underside of the arm with the second line.

I remember thinking how beautiful the words looked on my skin. Whorish for sure, a slutty lipstick red, but bold and honest at the same time; unashamed. Artistic and painterly. It was a color I had seen on a canvas at the Met or the Modern or maybe only in a book. Veronica turned me on to it, that I'm sure of. Big slabs of meat hanging at the butcher shop. I don't remember the artist's name. He passed away very young from what I can recall. After he died, his wife jumped out the window pregnant with his baby. His red was called *vermilion* and it had been banned by the dictator so he fled to Paris. Maybe his name was Chaim? I think he was an Italian Jew.

I kept on drinking and writing and at some point took my (his) pants off. I started on my legs and feet. When I had gotten through all twenty or so of the lyrics, I started from the beginning on my chest and stomach. I used big letters at first but when an area would get too crowded I would make the words very small. In some places where there was no room for an entire word, I would only write a letter or two. I covered my skin with as many words as was possible. I went into the bathroom and began to write on my face. I couldn't tell if the letters were backward or forward.

I stared at my face in the mirror.

I had succeeded beyond all expectations!

I realized it didn't matter if anyone could read the words because I had *become* the words. I was the song. The lyrics now incarnate: flesh, bones, and blood. I thought the transformation would have pleased Lou.

Back in the bedroom I took off my underwear and wrote the words *mask* and *stained* on and around my private parts. His words, not mine. I killed the gin. Then I stretched out flat on the floor, spit into my palm, and masturbated. I tried to think of Veronica's beautiful pale-white body. Small, thin, and naked. I kept seeing the rope around her neck so I imagined one rope with two loops. One for her and one for me. The more excited she got, the louder she screamed. The louder she screamed, the tighter the nooses got. The tighter the nooses got, the more excited she got.

It took a long time and a lot of effort but I finally made myself come. The words down there were a smudged-up mess; it looked like my dick was cut and bleeding. But I was too tired to clean myself and too drunk to care.

thirty-eight

I was sure I knew him from somewhere though I couldn't quite place the man. He was trying to wake me up but I was very sick. He shook me and tried to cover my body with my clothes but I kept shaking them off because I was so hot. He shouted at me in a foreign accent: "Boy! Hey, boy! Wake up, boy!"

It was daylight, morning I guess. My stomach was upset and I knew I was close to puking. Rogelio! That was his name. He worked in the building.

"Why you do this, boy? You can't stay here!"

I tried to get to my feet and run to the toilet but I was so dizzy the floor fell to a forty-five-degree angle and I was on my back again.

"Put the pants, boy. Put the clothes on." He said clothes in two syllables: *clo-thes*.

I turned my head away from him and puked on the floor. It spread out in an almost perfect circle. Rogelio jumped back to avoid the splatter but there was none. It was a contained and tidy spread of vomit. He clicked his tongue in disappointment.

"Put the clo-thes, boy! Please!"

I felt bad for him. I sat up and he handed me my pants. I had to lie down again. The room was spinning and I was going to be sick again. I needed water, I was so thirsty. I asked him for some and he left the room clicking his tongue. I closed my eyes and tried to stop the spins.

When I opened my eyes my mother was cleaning my face with a warm, wet towel. The towel was white but it turned pink very quickly. I was still naked and felt embarrassed that my mom was seeing me in the altogether but then I became aware that I was in the bathtub in my apartment. I was submerged up to my neck in a hot bubble bath and I wasn't so ashamed. The bubbles had swirls of pink and red—the remains of Lou's last song. Doomed to banishment down the drain, into the sewers of New York City, seeping into the harbor and washing up at the feet of Lady Liberty.

I asked my mother to make a copy of the words on Lou's wall. They were his last words, they were important and had to be preserved.

"Shhhh," she said as she gently scrubbed my chin. She told me to close my eyes and rest. Everything would be okay. Not to worry. Rest. You're home now. You're safe.

But my eyes were already closed. Weren't they? I was confused. I was not in the bathtub and my mother wasn't with me. I was still on Lou's bedroom floor.

I saw Rogelio to my left. His face was close to mine and he was trying to get me to sit up. I heard a crackling static sound and a woman's voice calling out a sequence of numbers and streets. Rogelio put a blanket over my shoulders. The woman's voice was coming out of a walkie-talkie that hung from a cop's belt. The cop was on my right side and he was helping Rogelio lift me up. There was a fireman in the room too. He was unfastening the belts of a stretcher on wheels. The cop had kind eyes and kept telling me to stay calm, everything would be okay. Not to worry. You're safe.

I was wheeled through Lou's empty apartment, then through the hallway and into the elevator. My mother was at my side by the time I was in the lobby. She was crying, hysterical and unraveled. I was very sorry to have done this to her. She rode with me in the ambulance and held my hand. Neither one of us said a word.

thirty-nine

"GUY WALKS INTO A MENTAL HOSPITAL"
A Comedy in One Act and 180 Days

PLACE: Adolescent psych ward of an NYC Hospital.
TIME: The present. Or past or future. Take your pick.
CAST: Dr. X, a middle-aged shrink from South America.
Kid Y: A seventeen-year-old boy from Queens.

ACT 1

IT IS VERY EARLY IN THE MORNING AND DR. X IS
INTERVIEWING KID Y IN HIS OFFICE. DR. X REFERS
TO AN OPEN FILE ON HIS DESK.

DR. X: What were you feeling when you started to write all these things on your body?

KID Y: I was preserving what I thought may have been the last lyrics written by a famous rock star.

DR. X: And this "rock star," you know him personally?

KID Y: Yes. I was in his apartment.

DR. X: The apartment was empty. There was no one living there.

KID Y: He moved out.

DR. X: Why were you in his empty apartment?

KID Y: He was a friend of mine. I went to visit him.

DR. X: If he was your friend, why didn't he tell you he was moving?

KID Y: I don't know.

DR. X: Did you write on your body first or the wall first?

KID Y: I didn't write on the wall. My friend did.

DR. X: The rock star?

KID Y: Yes.

DR. X: Why would he write on the wall?

KID Y: I don't know, you'd have to ask him.

DR. X: Does this rock star have a name?

KID Y: Lou Reed.

DR. X: I've never heard of him. Maybe he's not such a star.

KID Y: Maybe not.

DR. X: Maybe he's a star in your own mind.

KID Y: No, he has a following.

DR. X: Are you one of his followers?

KID Y: I was his friend.

DR. X: Was?

KID Y: Well, he's gone.

DR. X: Where did he go?

KID Y: I have no idea.

PAUSE

DR. X: Did he tell you to write the words on your body?

KID Y: No.

DR. X: You did it under your own volition?

KID Y: Yes.

DR. X: Does he ever tell you to do things?

KID Y: Well, he's asked me to do things. He didn't really tell me to do them. I had a choice.

DR. X: What did he ask of you?

KID Y: Oh . . . let's see . . . He wanted me to take dictation but that never happened.

DR. X: He wanted to dictate what you did, give you orders?

KID Y: No, no . . . he wanted me to help him write. He was writing a play.

DR. X: Was he a rock star or a playwright?

KID Y: I guess he was a rock star who was writing a play.

DR. X: And he needed your help.

KID Y: No. I think he just didn't like being alone.

DR. X: Do you like being alone?

KID Y: Sometimes.

DR. X: (reading from a page of the file) "If you need someone to kill I'm a man without a will." Whose words are those?

KID Y: Those were the words he wrote on the wall. I think they were the lyrics to a song.

DR. X: That's a very strange song, don't you think?

KID Y: Not if you knew him.

PAUSE

DR. X: Tell me about Victoria.

KID Y: Victoria who?

DR. X: Your friend who took her own life.

KID Y: Veronica.

DR. X: Yes. I'm sorry. Veronica. Tell me about her.

KID Y: She was very smart, very pretty . . . creative . . . kind.

DR. X: Were you in love with her?

KID Y: Yes.

DR. X: It must have been difficult for you to lose her.

KID Y: It was.

DR. X: After she did what she did, did you want to do the same?

KID Y: No.

DR. X: But you told my colleague that you would be surprised if you made it to your eighteenth birthday.

KID Y: I did say that and I still feel that way.

DR. X: Because you are a danger to yourself?

KID Y: No.

DR. X: Then why did you say that?

KID Y: I don't know . . . I just feel a sense of impending doom.

DR. X: Did you write the words on your body because of what happened to Victoria?

KID Y: Veronica.

DR. X: Sorry. Yes. Veronica.

KID Y: No. I wrote Lou's words, his lyrics, which he had written on his wall, on my body because I couldn't find a piece of paper.

DR. X: Is that the truth?

KID Y: Yes. Lou was gone, he moved out and I had a bad feeling about it so I thought it was important to preserve his song for posterity in case he was dead. But I really had no reason to believe he was dead, just that day I was thinking maybe it was possible he had killed himself because his girlfriend had left him and the last time I saw him he was so depressed. Plus, I was feeling that sense of impending doom like I told you. So if these were really his last words, I felt somebody should write them down because the apartment was probably going to be painted soon and the wall where he wrote the song would be covered over.

DR. X: He was depressed because his girlfriend left him?

KID Y: Yes. But she wasn't a girl, really. I think she was a guy who looked like a girl and dressed like a girl and Lou treated him, treated her like a girl. So did I. I considered her a girl.

LONG PAUSE. DR. X WRITES IN THE FILE
THEN READS FROM THE NEXT PAGE.

DR. X: "Dirty's what you are and clean is what you're not." Do you feel that you are dirty, and not clean?

KID Y: No.

DR. X: Then why did you write it on yourself?

KID Y: Third base.

DR. X: What?

KID Y: Third base. Who's on first? It's an Abbott and Costello routine.

DR. X: What's that?

KID Y: A comedy routine.

DR. X: Ahhhh. So you think it was funny when you wrote on yourself?

KID Y: Not at all.

DR. X: Do you want to be a rock star?

KID Y: I have no musical abilities.

DR. X: What if this rock star does not exist?

KID Y: There's people you can ask about him. The doorman of the building. Go to a record store. He exists, he's real.

DR. X: Yes. Yes. We will look into all of this. We shall. Very soon.

KID Y: I heard Allen Ginsberg was a patient here and stayed in my room. Is that true?

DR. X: That would be confidential.

KID Y: Of course.

DR. X: Judy Garland was here, though. And Lenny Bruce.

KID Y: They're not confidential?

DR. X: They're dead.

DR. X CLOSES THE FILE.

DR. X: Okay, Matthew, that's all for today. (Dr. X grins.) Maybe all we have to do is just give you a head transplant and send you on your way.

PAUSE

KID Y: Do I get to approve the donor?

THE LIGHTS GO TO BLACK. IF THERE IS A CURTAIN (THERE SHOULD BE), IT SHOULD COME DOWN NOW.

forty

I was told that my scores on the tests were some of the highest they had ever seen. I am not sure if that is something to be proud of or not. I did not ask for clarification and did not care to know what it actually meant. Whether I was the most brilliant kid to ever visit their fine establishment or the most crazy did not matter in the least; I was going to be sticking around awhile. The things I wrote on myself were being used against me to establish that I was "a risk to others or myself." That meant I had to be kept off the streets.

Manic episode . . . angel/demon delusions . . . schizoid tendencies . . . these are among the words I overheard from those who are supposed to know who is and who is not a proper fit for the highly organized, well-ordered, and functional society we live in.

I think my big mistake was revealing to them my fears that I was the victim of some kind of witchcraft or spell and under the influence of various nefarious curses and hexes. I both believed this 100 percent and did not believe it at all. I gave them no specific names or details as to who put this upon me or precisely how I was afflicted by it. I regret saying any of this at all and I know it really did me in as far as my case for going home went.

"Just do your time, don't think too much, keep your body clean, eat whatever they give you, take your medicine, and you'll sail outta here fit and happy before you know it." This was told to me by an orderly named Roscoe.

I like Roscoe better than anyone else on the staff. He is the kindest and in my opinion the smartest and the most honest. Every once in a while he'll give me an Almond Joy or an *Archie* comic book from his personal collection.

I've followed his advice as much as possible.

Roscoe was born in Oxford, Mississippi, which I told him was the home of William Faulkner. Roscoe had never heard of him. Later on, as we became closer, he confided in me that his father had been lynched by the Ku Klux Klan when he was five years old. His dad was accused of cheating a white man out of ten bales of hay so the Klan burned their trademark cross in front of their house. Roscoe's dad refused to be intimidated because he had done nothing wrong. A week later he was founded swinging from a sweet gum tree in a grove near Ole Miss. After the funeral, Roscoe's mom moved him and his sisters up to Memphis where he spent most of his childhood.

Roscoe was of great help to me in explaining how the medicine was going to affect me. In the beginning I was afraid it would dull my mind, soften and blur all my edges, and leave me wandering (waddling?) in a permanent fuzzy haze like some of the other kids in here. Roscoe assured me that I might feel a little sluggish for a while but that would pass as my body and mind got used to the dosage.

It was pretty miserable in the beginning. My body felt like shit and I didn't feel like talking very much. But somewhere in the middle of July I started to feel better.

After the first long weeks during which I was allowed no visitors, my mother finally came to see me. I'm not sure what I looked like then, but it must have been awful because she kept rubbing my cheeks and straightening my posture. She fixed my hair too, wetting her fingers with saliva, rubbing her hands together, and then smoothing out the cowlicks atop my head.

Actually, Mom came to sign me out but she quickly learned that it wasn't an option and wouldn't be for some time. I think she felt very guilty, as if it were somehow her fault. I tried to smile to let her know I would be okay, though I'm not sure if what I was thinking and intending in my head translated properly to the muscles in my face.

The next day Mom brought me some books and the latest issue of *MAD* magazine. Its cover had a drawing of King Kong scratching his head as he looked at his lady who sat knitting in the palm of his hand. I had been reading *MAD* since I was nine so forgive her the irony, please, bless her heart. She was doing whatever she could to hold herself together under the circumstances. I think she was taking the whole thing worse than I was.

She explained to me that the books had been given to her by my principal at Hobart and that he'd arranged with her an accelerated course of study for me while I was away from school. She asked if I was okay with the idea.

I squeezed her hand and tried to smile. "Sure," I said.

"Mr. Barrett said you might even be able to graduate early if you can keep up with what he gives you. What do you think of that?"

Under the circumstances I didn't see how that was possible. I felt we were putting the cart way in front of the horse but I didn't let her see my doubts. I squeezed her hand again, she kissed and hugged me goodbye.

She left a bag of underwear, socks, and T-shirts

on my bed and the books stacked tall on my desk: *Of Mice and Men*, *To Kill a Mockingbird*, *1984*, *Animal Farm*, *The Stranger*, *The Diary of Anne Frank*, *Invisible Man*, and *Candide*.

It was an impressive list and I would eventually get to reading all of them. They had a lot in common: prejudice, intolerance, cruelty, persecution of the other, subjugation of the weak, the powerful dominating the meek, evil triumphing over good, genocide, murder, and slavery. All the lovely themes that keep repeating themselves over the course of recorded history.

The other book I read during this period was the Bible. It was provided by the hospital and was freely available to all who wanted it. All of the above-mentioned themes were also featured in the Bible alongside the familiar litany of human sacrifice, plagues, locusts, floods, torture, and crucifixion.

I was getting an education in the march of human progress and it seemed that if we are to be certain of any one thing at all, it's that most of us are lambs waiting to be slaughtered at the hands of the butchers. A realization made far worse by the fact that the butchers are invariably idiotic, pea-brained morons whose stupidity almost manages to overshadow their cruelty. Almost.

Paradoxically, being aware of all this has given me great strength and courage. The devil as you know it. It's like everything makes much more sense to me now. As if the veils have been lifted and behind the curtain there is just the truth, naked and raw, in sharp focus, with all the details defined.

I have come to a real understanding of who Lou was, who Veronica was, and why they were who they were. Why they did what they did.

It all comes down to a particular and special quality they shared. I call it *an acute sensitivity to human fragility.* I think it was something that became unbearable to them quite often so they were forced to find ways of coping with it. This was achieved in two ways: one, by covering themselves in layers of armor; and two, by transmuting it into music (in Lou's case) or words (in Veronica's, though never fully realized).

In the end Lou's armor proved to be much thicker.

It reminds me of the famous words, *What does not kill me makes me stronger.* Veronica was very fond of this quote by Nietzsche. I hope it proves true in my case.

Then again, wasn't it Nietzsche who also said: *Whom the gods would destroy, they first make mad?*

I'm pretty sure it was Nietzsche.

But maybe I'm wrong.

Maybe it wasn't him.

Maybe it was Alfred E. Neuman.

forty-one

I finally finished the letter I began in Veronica's backyard. Truth is, I never got beyond *Dear Veronica* that
day beneath the fire escape. All I need to do now is
sign it and it will be official. Forever.

Dear Veronica:

*Forgive me for not conjuring your image in my
mind for long stretches of time and for the days that
pass without thoughts of you or wishes for your peaceful rest or a better rebirth or protection from the lord of
death and his legions of doom.*

*Only two months gone and the hours, days, and
weeks are already filled with things other than the tre-
mendous loss I felt when you passed. The inertia, pa-
ralysis, and grief that hung about me have disappeared.
My mind has released itself from the burden of your absence and I feel like a shitheel because of it.*

And I threw away the necklace you gave me.

*Forgive me for not having your face permanently
emblazoned in my brain anymore. I had hoped you
would be there always without pause, in my thoughts*

constantly for years, my mourning and sorrow continuous for decade upon decade.

But here it is, only eight weeks later, and I'm over it. How awful and unkind. How selfish, egoistic, and disgusting of me.

Last week I was sitting by the window and a bus drove by. Its exhaust blended with the smell of the rain on asphalt and I was instantly transported to the very first time I stood outside your building. Waiting outside the door for you to come down after your voice, breathless and hurried, came through the intercom and said: "One minute."

The memory hung clear for a few seconds and then narrowed in focus into smaller and smaller circles of vision, shrinking all the way down to the size and shape of a peephole and then gone. I slept sound and dreamless and woke up rested without a thought or picture of you. Forgive me, please.

What would you say in response to this? Would you say I'm human? It's human . . . it's natural . . . it's to be expected? Or would you say I'm a monster? Cold, heartless, uncaring, and that's how it's always been with me and always would have been? Or maybe it's none of the above? Maybe it's . . . maybe I . . . maybe . . .

Yours Always,

forty-two

My mother was very excited the other day. She told me I may be able to get my diploma before Christmas if I keep doing the work I've been doing. It was good to see her happy. The poor thing has been through so much. I asked her about final exams and she said they won't be necessary, I just have to keep completing the work she brings me every week. I am convinced my mother wrote the school a big check. Next year there will probably be a plaque on a desk somewhere in my school with my grandfather's name on it.

Mom also brought some brochures for colleges (Boston College, Columbia, and Fordham). This took me by surprise. I hadn't been thinking much about college. I'm not planning on going anytime soon and was hoping to take a year (maybe two) off, but she thinks it couldn't hurt to start exploring options. I don't know. Not sure what I want to do besides get the fuck out of here.

I turn eighteen soon and will be moved upstairs to the adult ward. My mother has hatched a plan, bless her heart. She is convinced that the head of security has a crush on her and she thinks she can enlist his help and get me out of here so we can celebrate my birthday someplace special. She whispered all this in my ear in view of the nurses and orderlies. She was holding me tight, pretending to hug me, but revealing her caper in detail.

She thinks she can get Mr. Ruffalo, the security chief, to leave the rear stairwell door unlocked for a ten-minute span right after lights-out on Friday. I would slip downstairs and out the emergency door where my mother would be waiting in a limousine. She would have packed a suitcase for me and we would go straight to the airport and fly to Italy to visit Rome and Naples. Two cities she's always wanted to see. We'd tour the Vatican and the excavated city of Pompeii.

I didn't want to burst her bubble but I reminded her that neither one of us had a passport and there was no way to leave the country without one. She suggested Miami as an alternative. I squeezed her tight and told her that if I escaped it would work against me and they would probably keep me here longer. And that it would be best to go to Miami or maybe even Italy *after* my release, which looks like it will be before the holidays.

I haven't shaved since I've been here and I have a scraggly black beard. When I see myself in the mirror it doesn't look like me. Not the me I remember as me. I look more like the man in the only postcard Veronica ever sent me. It was a self-portrait of Picasso as a young man. During his blue period, I think. She wrote on the back of it, *Matt, you are so much more than you think you are, and so much less than me. Ha ha ha! Just kidding. Happy 17th. Veronica. P.S. If you grew a beard you might look like this. Think about it.*

My best friend here is a girl named Nicole. She plays Bach and Brahms on the flute. They only allow her to play one hour in the morning and one hour in the evening. The rest of the time they keep the flute locked up. God knows why a flute would need incarceration but those are the rules here at the Waldorf Hysteria.

When Nicole plays her face gets clear and quiet, like a serious child. But when she's just hanging out she can be wicked and sarcastic in a very funny way. And she knows the filthiest jokes.

I think I might be in love.

I want to come clean. I really do. I have nothing left to hide.

afterwords

California, November 2013

I'm heading up the 101 with Los Angeles behind me. I think it's autumn. It's night so it's hard to tell. It's hard to tell in the daytime too. The sun has no seasons in Southern California. Or maybe it does and I just haven't figured them out yet.

On the edge of Thousand Oaks I find myself at the top of the Conejo Grade. It's a dizzying decline that twists down into the valley where Camarillo begins. If you didn't know any better you could easily think you were about to fall off the edge of the world.

This stretch of Cali freeway is supposedly haunted by the ghost of a hitchhiking migrant farmworker who was run over by a drunken teenager who hung himself in his jail cell. Which I suppose makes two ghosts, though it's only the farmhand who's been seen in these parts.

And though I have no idea where in the Los Angeles area my father crashed and burned, something in my gut tells me it was here. I'm sure there are ways to research it and find out the truth, but I have yet to do so and probably never will. Sometimes the truth of imagination is easier to live with than the truth of fact.

By day you can see hills rolling on for miles, some of them strange and mysterious, like flattop pyramids grown over wild—too correct in angle and line to be a product of nature. At night it's like sitting in the cockpit of an airplane as you slowly descend to a narrow landing strip between the mountains, hills, farmland, and the lights of the Camarillians. Depending on which way the wind is blowing, you might get a heady waft of peaty fertilizer or sugary strawberry if luck is with you.

But tonight the air is still. One of your songs comes on the radio. You are only a few days dead so a lot of your songs are being sent over the airwaves. It's an old song, one of your earliest. A nugget that would spawn so many more of its kind as an unbroken chain of admirers fell under your influence.

It's a tender tune. A sad, slow song, sweet and delicate. Something churns in my solar plexus and threatens release through the eyes. It catches me by surprise, then it breaks and the tears come. Big drops that fall out easy. They drip like wax, sealing all the oaths and pledges. It feels good.

I go from surprise to shock when I notice it's

raining. It hasn't rained here in years but the sky doesn't know that so it sends the water down as if it were common. It pours like the tropics and it's very hard to see. Dangerous. West Coast drivers are unaccustomed to wet roads and impaired visibility. We all slow to a steady creep, some of us crying.

I cry as much for your passing as I do for the time unrecoverable that has passed me by. I cry for the boy I was, who became a man. For the city I loved, which has vanished like you have. For the beautiful, brilliant shooting starlet who left this earth while still a child. I cry for never having known you once I was old enough to understand who you really were and the magnitude of the art you made.

The story told here, closing with me on the edge of manhood, is as much yours as it is mine. Its end is where we parted and it would be at least fifteen years until I'd see you again.

I didn't mention who I was or that we'd met before because I didn't expect you'd remember or recognize me. You didn't. So I expressed my admiration as a fan.

I'm pretty sure it was a postpremiere party for a film and I'm certain it was at El Teddy's or El Internacionale. I don't recall what incarnation the joint was at the time. You were standing at one of the floor-length urinals in the men's room. After following you in (I know), I stood and peed—with an empty drain between us to be polite.

Looking straight ahead at the white-tiled wall, I said: "I was listening to you this afternoon. 'Magic and Loss.' It's a masterpiece."

You glanced over for a little second and after assessing if I posed any threat, you turned back to the wall and said kindly: "That's pretty cool." Then you zipped up and walked away.

A little while later I watched you drinking a can of Tecate at the bar. This surprised me because word on the street was that you were anonymously sober. Standing next to my recovering friend whose guest I was that evening, I pointed out the beer. He shrugged and said: "Junkies, man. They have a sobriety all their own."

I didn't understand what he meant.

By then you were a long way from junk or speed or whatever it was that possessed you way back when. And to reduce you to *junkie*, like, *Once a junkie, always a junkie*—well, for my friend I apologize.

I was happy to see you sip the beer. It made me see clear the fluid and idiosyncratic possibilities in our lives, or maybe more accurately: the fluidity and idiosyncrasy that *is* our lives. It made me see that there are escape routes out of hell and if we are fortunate we can make a clean getaway and survive.

We survived the fires that started when we kicked the candles in our sleep, too fucked up to remember to blow them out. We survived the fights at dawn when there was nothing left to say but curses, low-blow insults, and the revelations of harbored desires to inflict violence and pain. We survived falling down the stone stairs backward, literally head over heels, because we were so drunk and the last cigarette made us so dizzy. Yes, we were lucky and earned that sip of beer at the bar.

The next time I saw you was ten years after the men's-room encounter. You were performing at the second permutation of the Knitting Factory. It was the first April of the new millennium and you had just released a new album. Four decades in and your work was as potent, relevant, and necessary as anyone's, if not more so. I remember thinking as you walked onstage that you were the same age my father would have been; just about sixty. It would be the only time I would ever see you perform live and the last time I would ever be in your presence.

What I proceeded to behold that evening was the living embodiment of rock and roll itself. Its essence distilled and offered up with generosity and benevolence for all those who gathered to bear witness to the passion; to the majesty, ferocity, and might. The power and the glory. Transmitted through vibration, gesture, and mind (mantra, mudra, and meditation), from you to us with love and compassion. For we know not what we do.

And more than anything else, it was punk. Which should come as no surprise since you were its creator. I don't care what Detroit says, you were doing it when Iggy was a mere Osterberg and Kramer was trying to figure out who the other four would be. As for the lads from my neck of the woods (famous for their "*One, two, three, four*" count-off and three power chords) who are considered by some as the progenitors of the movement . . . well, that just makes no sense chronologically or otherwise. Not to mention (but I will) that they basically wrote the same song over and over again. And however great a song it may be, it renders deep catalog cuts redundant. Sorry, kids, I guess you had to be there—on the Bowery when it happened. But I wasn't.

And the same goes for the little London boy. Just the first few sentences you speak to the audience on *Take No Prisoners* relegates John-John to a corner with some crayons and a finger up his nose. The revolution you started was one of art and intellect. It inspired the defeat of tyranny in Czechoslovakia, for Christ's sake. God save the queen, indeed.

The song ends and the tears stop as suddenly as they

started. Another song of yours begins to play. It's the one that got me into all the trouble. You played it that night at the Knitting Factory, a miracle really, because I loved it so much and it was rarely included in your live repertoire. It was sheer delight that evening and maybe even more thrilling tonight.

It opens with a wail (your guitar), then it churns and rumbles (bass and drums), then melts euphoric (more guitar), then you shout. It is heroic and brave. Transcendent and holy.

And it doesn't look like the rain will stop.

I hit the gas hard and head into the West.

Acknowledgments

I am forever grateful to: my dear parents Dan and Claire, my brother John, Ryszard and Raisa Chlebowski, His Eminence Garchen Rinpoche, Elijah Amitin, Laurie Anderson, Sharon Angela, Jean-Claude Baker, Norena Barbella, Valerie Baugh, Jack Cacamis, Seymour Cassel, Bruno de Almeida, John Frey, Roger Haber, Tom Gilroy, Fernando Gomes, Ti Jean, Joe Laurita, Richard Lewis, Gary Lippman, Steven P. Morrissey, Joyce Carol Oates, Nick Sandow, Joe Scarpinito, Steve Schirripa, Richard Sottosanti, Johnny Temple and Akashic Books, Tina Thor and TMT Entertainment, Olmo Tighe, Mark Turgeon, John Ventimiglia, Francine Volpe, my agents at ICM: Hrishi Desai, Dan Kirschen, and Ruthanne Secunda.

And of course . . . to the incomparable Lou Reed, for his kindness and for all the beautiful art.

Swoop, swoop, rock, rock